W9-BHW-597

OTHER

Harlequin Romances

by MARY WHISTLER

Many of these titles are available at your local bookseller,
or through the Harlequin Reader Service.

For a free catalogue listing all available Harlequin Romances,
send your name and address to:

HARLEQUIN READER SERVICE,
M.P.O. Box 707, Niagara Falls, N.Y. 14302
Canadian address: Stratford, Ontario, Canada.

or use order coupon at back of book.

PATHWAY OF ROSES

by

MARY WHISTLER

HARLEQUIN   BOOKS

TORONTO   ●   WINNIPEG

First published in 1962 by Mills & Boon Limited,
17 - 19 Foley Street, London, England

SBN 373-01550-X

© Mary Whistler 1962

Harlequin Canadian edition published December, 1971
Harlequin U.S. edition published March, 1972

CHAPTER I

OLD Hermann Brandt lifted the violin out of its case and touched it tenderly.

"This was not made yesterday, no," he murmured, as he so often did. "Not the creation of one of the master craftsmen, but a fine instrument." He ran the bow across the responsive strings, and his whole face lighted with pleasure. "Did you hear that, Janie? That is music, yes?"

Janie agreed with him, and looked almost as enthusiastic.

"Play something," she begged, but he shook his head and put the violin away again in its case, and returned the case to the shelf.

"No, there is much to do, and I cannot spare the time." He sighed as he contemplated the array— or rather, the disarray—in front of him. "Why is it that we collect so much junk, Janie, and only a very little of that which is truly valuable?" He picked up a battered mouth-organ, and then cast it aside to join company with a selection of flutes, trumpets, accordions, etc. The whole tiny shop seemed to be full of the discarded accompaniments of a musician's life. "Even a poor violin gives me pleasure, but I have never yet attempted to play on a mouth-organ!"

He turned away, suddenly very businesslike, and a little peevish.

"Those lists, those lists," he demanded petulantly. "That latest consignment of gramophone records? Pick of the Pops!" and he actually snorted. "Have you got them all sorted, and on display to our customers?"

One of the customers, a youth in too-tight trousers and an amazing sweater, came in and bought a couple of the latest records, and Janie put his money inside the till, and gave him the right amount of change. When he had gone away, and the shop door-bell had stopped quivering, she returned to her employer's side and watched him flicking aimlessly with a feather duster at a bust of Beethoven that stood on a pedestal in a corner.

"You had good news this morning?" she asked him, very softly, because she knew that he had received a letter. "Your daughter is well, Mr. Brandt?"

He shook his head, staring owlishly at the bust of Beethoven.

"Not so well, child. She has a bad throat . . . a tired throat, she calls it. She is coming home on a visit. Just a short visit."

"Oh, but that's wonderful!" Janie exclaimed, amazed that he didn't appear to think so. "Even a short visit will mean that you will actually see her, and be able to talk with her. And I expect a good many famous singers suffer from tired throats occasionally. And after such an exhausting tour ——"

"She says that it went off well," the old man remarked, as if it was of little interest to him. "She says that every time she sang the audience rose to its feet and cheered her until they were hoarse. In Vienna there were so many bouquets that her dressing-room was like a corner of an enchanted garden." He studied Janie as if there were certain aspects of her appearance that were striking him for the first time. "You have hair the same colour as hers . . . so very fair! Your eyes are grey, and hers are as blue as a summer sky, but otherwise you are much alike. I am surprised that I haven't noticed it before."

Janie smiled at him.

"You flatter me," she told him. "I've seen photographs of your daughter, don't forget, and there can only be one Vanessa Brandt in the whole wide world."

He sighed again.

"She was christened Sophia," he remarked. "I do not know why she should call herself Vanessa."

"For publicity reasons, I expect. Because it sounds good."

"Sophia is a family name," he muttered obstinately. "To me it also sounds very good indeed, and how are my neighbours to know that I have a famous daughter if she calls herself by some other name?"

"Ah," Janie accused him, as she took the feather duster out of his hand before he could flick most of the objects on an upper shelf off it and on to the floor. "So it's your vanity that is suffering most this morning, is it? Because you can't boast of her, and stick a notice in the window informing everyone that Sophia is coming home! But you can prepare for her coming and bake a cake. Or your housekeeper can. . . ." She turned him gently towards the door to an inner room, and then gave him a push. "Go and tell her to kill the fatted calf, and we'll put the flags out afterwards!"

Old Hermann mumbled to himself.

"Sophia will not want that. Sophia will come back here like a thief in the night and wish that no one shall see her! She always hated this street, and how will such as she appreciate one of my good Flora's cakes?"

Janie stared at him in a certain amount of surprise. She had only worked for Hermann Brandt for six months, but the one thing she really knew about him was that he adored his daughter . . . his only daughter. She was beautiful, and at twenty-six she was a well-known coloratura soprano. She had escaped from the little world of narrow streets and unpretentious houses in which she had been born and brought up and became a star that twinkled in a brighter world . . . a more expensive world, where some of the houses that offered her hospitality were near-palaces, and their owners people with titles who would look down on little men like Hermann Brandt as very ordinary little men indeed. In spite of his ability to recognize a Stradivarius even if it were about to disintegrate into dust, and his fine long-fingered hands that could restore it if restoration were possible.

She had escaped . . . and apparently she wasn't eager to return!

That was another thing Janie had just learned about her, although somehow she couldn't believe it. She tried to reassure Hermann.

"But of course she's just longing to get back and see you and her old home. I don't suppose she's had much opportunity until now. . . ." She watched him start to climb the staircase that led to the flat above the shop. "When do you expect to see her?"

Hermann shrugged.

"It could be any time now. She said that she was flying home, and aeroplanes travel quickly."

She actually arrived that afternoon, when Janie was still busily engaged in listing the latest consignment of gramophone records. She pushed open the door of the shop and the unharmonious bell jangled so harshly that Janie looked up, almost startled. A taxi was gliding away from the kerb, and the rain was slanting downwards and making the roads glisten. Vanessa Brandt was so beautifully dressed, and so much more than beautiful herself, that Janie knew at once who she was. She stood up, pushing back her chair.

Vanessa directed a glacial blue look at her.

"Who are you?" she demanded curtly.

Janie explained.

"I'm Mr. Brandt's assistant. . . . Your *father's* assistant?" she queried, certain she could not be wrong.

Vanessa didn't condescend to answer. She merely walked right in and started looking disdainfully about the shop.

CHAPTER II

JANIE put away the lists of gramophone records. She watched Vanessa studying the contents of the shop with curiosity, that strong suspicion of contempt that was in every line of her features.

She had astonishingly delicate features, and for one with humble beginnings, remarkably patrician ones. They suggested a pale and flawless cameo with curling lips and sensitive nostrils, and her eyes were very large and cold and blue. Her hair was pale guinea gold, and was trained to wind itself smoothly about her elegantly poised head, and to lie in a knot on the nape of her neck. The hat she wore, which was very captivating, had a wisp of some sort of veiling which emphasized the porcelain delicacy of her appearance.

"So my father has not conquered his weakness for acquiring rubbish," she remarked, as she spurned the battered musical instruments with a solitary glance.

"It's not because he admires rubbish," Janie felt forced to reply, "but because he always feels so sorry for the people who want to sell it to him." Vanessa's eyes rested on her thoughtfully.

"And you, no doubt, work for him for a pittance because you are in sympathy with his philanthrophic ideas of how to run a business," she stated rather than asked. Then: "Where is he?" she wanted to know.

"Upstairs," Janie told her. "At least, so far as I know."

"Preparing to welcome me home?" with a kind of brittle dryness.

"I've no doubt he's fairly actively concerned with a certain amount of preparation for your homecoming," was the careful response to that.

Vanessa whipped the captivating little hat from off her head, and cast it down on the counter with a sigh of relief. She ran slim fingers through the soft gold of her hair, loosening it, and then sat down in the only available chair and opened her handbag. She produced a toy of a cigarette case of gold and tortoiseshell and selected a cigarette and lighted it.

"I'm not in any hurry for that sort of thing," she confessed. "And if I won't be in your way I'll sit here for a bit." She closed her eyes, as if she was mentally and physically exhausted, while she drew abstractedly on the cigarette; and then, when she opened them again, there was a curious alert look in them as she fixed them upon Janie. "You're pretty," she observed. "You're very pretty for a backwater like this. Why do you work here?"

"Because I like it here," Janie replied with simplicity.

"You mean you actually enjoy working in all this muddle?"

"I try to straighten it up sometimes," Janie informed her, with a smile. "But I honestly believe your father prefers a muddle, because he soon sees to it that we're in a state of chaos again! However, he's a musician, and you can't expect a musician to be orderly."

"I'm a singer, and I love order," Vanessa corrected her sharply. "I escaped from this kind of life because I had a superior voice, and I can't remember a single moment of my life when I was happy here. Does that surprise you?"

"No," Janie answered, looking at her. "Not really."

"Have you ever heard me sing?" Vanessa inquired, with an arrogant tilt to her chin.

Janie nodded.

"We have several recordings of yours here in the shop. Your father is very proud of them," she added.

"So he should be," the other commented, looking mildly pleased. "I've climbed a long way since the days when he tried to teach me the piano. Actually, I never did learn to play very well, but my voice . . . my voice has been described as the voice of a nightingale!" Her blue eyes remained triumphantly fixed on Janie's face. "That's something, isn't it?"

"It is indeed," Janie agreed.

Vanessa crushed out her cigarette in the ashtray. She swallowed, as if something was hurting her throat, and then coughed a little.

"I shouldn't smoke," she admitted. "I've been ill . . . or rather, I'm very tired, and I've got to undergo an operation. Oh, nothing to worry about, but it's a nuisance . . . a particular nuisance just now." She seemed quite fascinated by the girl in the pink overall, who was automatically doing things with her hands all the time that she was talking. Neatly clipping thin strips of paper that looked like invoices together, and then tucking them away in a drawer. Sorting the disorder in the drawer. "You know," she remarked suddenly, "you're not at all unlike me."

Janie stared at her.

"That's the sort of compliment I hardly feel I deserve, Miss Brandt."

Vanessa made a gesture with her hand.

"I'm not complimenting you, I'm merely remarking on something that's a little extraordinary. If you and I were sisters the world could accept it that I'm the beautiful sister, and you're the slightly plainer one. But with grooming and so forth you could probably look ten times more attractive. And if someone took away that pink overall, and

dressed you in some fabulous creation of Dior's...."
Her voice trailed away, but her eyes were full of
speculation. "Do you know anything at all about
music?" she asked.

Janie replied with a somewhat dry note in her
own voice this time.

"I'm not a singer, Miss Brandt, if that's what
you mean. In addition," she added, "to bearing a
slight resemblance to you!"

"It's not slight," Vanessa told her. "It's remark-
able! The only serious difference is in the colour of
the eyes." She lighted another cigarette, as if she
needed it. "And of course I didn't mean can you
sing. You'd hardly be likely to have a voice like
mine, even if you did," with lofty disdain. "But if
you know something about music ... if you can talk
to people who make it their life, for instance; if
you are familiar with the various operas, could
identify a passage from some obscure symphony,
as well as being perfectly familiar with all the well-
known composers—well, then, you're a find indeed!"

"I go to the opera whenever I can afford it, and
I love Chopin," Janie told her, with a queer little
smile that had in it the merest hint of a form of
contempt. "Is that any use?" she inquired flip-
pantly.

"I think it could be of amazing use," Vanessa
said slowly, as if she could hardly believe in her

good fortune. Once more she crushed out a parti- ally smoked cigarette. "Listen," she said, "this is the set-up. This is the 'inside story', shall we say? I have to undergo an operation—a throat opera- tion—as I told you, and according to the surgeon the whole thing shouldn't take longer than a week. But by some unfortunate stroke of ill luck it hap- pens to be a very vital week for me . . . a week when I·simply have to be seen and heard and mix with people. I've been offered something quite wonder- ful in Vienna that calls for a tip-top bill of health, and the very maximum of energy and vitality— to say nothing of endurance!—and the man who is making me this offer wants to see me in New York in a few days' time. I'm supposed to be on my way there now, but I'm actually on my way to the hos- pital . . . I *daren't* postpone this operation any longer if my voice isn't to fail me altogether! And I've been at my wits' end trying to think up some- thing that could save the situation for me."

"I'm sorry," Janie said sincerely, "if the situa- tion is as bad as that."

"And you'll help me?" Vanessa demanded quickly, her whole being revitalized because an idea had dawned at last. "You're so like me no one would guess . . . certainly not anyone who hadn't really seen me very well before! And Abraham Winterton has never seen me before. He'll throw parties for me, introduce me to his friends . . . and offer me a fine fat contract!" She was fairly bubbling over. "And you won't have to sing a note, only *talk!*"

Janie looked, and felt, aghast.

"But you must be mad, Miss Brandt!" she protested. "Such a piece of deception is impossible. It wouldn't get by for a moment——"

"Don't be silly, my dear, it's a wonderful idea! And I'll have you fitted out with a whole new wardrobe. . . . As a matter of fact, we're much of a size, so you can wear some of my things. And Max Veldon will be at your elbow . . . give you all the support you'll need."

"Max Veldon?" Janie queried weakly. "The conductor?"

Vanessa smiled.

"To me he is something rather more than a conductor . . . although he is, of course, one of the most famous conductors in the world. He and I. . . ." Then she decided to say no more.

Janie twined her fingers together agitatedly.

"Miss Brandt," she pleaded. "Please forget this absurd notion. It wouldn't work—it couldn't work! —and, in any case, I couldn't have anything to do with it."

But Vanessa's blue eyes had a strangely hypnotizing effect.

"If you won't do this thing for me, you'll do it for my father, won't you?" she said. "I can tell

you're very fond of my father, and he made a lot
of sacrifices for me when I was young. I want to do
a lot of things for him"—she sent one of her con-
temptuous glances round the shop—"remove him
from this hovel, and I can do that if I get the Winterton contract." It was on the tip of Janie's
tongue to ask why she hadn't done anything for
her father before, but the words wouldn't frame
on her lips. And Vanessa went on with unnatural
persuasiveness: "And besides . . . think what an
interlude it will be for you! You must lead one of
the dullest lives of any girl I've ever known, and
I'm offering you a chance to escape . . . a chance to
see something of a world you know nothing about.
A world of brilliance and music."

Janie shook her head.

"I'm happy here."

"But you love music," coaxingly. "You go to the
opera whenever you can afford it, and you love
Chopin. In New York, for one brief and memorable week, you'll be caught up in a world of
music . . . you'll have it for breakfast, lunch and
dinner, if you want it. And you'll meet people . . .
all sorts of exciting new people. There'll be glamour—the glamour of smart clothes, cocktail parties,
night-clubs. . . ."

"No," Janie said.

Vanessa spoke deliberately.

"Have you ever seen Max Veldon conduct?"

"Once," Janie answered, and felt her knees grow weak. She had never forgotten the night she watched Max Veldon conduct, and heard a famous orchestra give of its best.

"He's quite devastating, isn't he?" Vanessa murmured, with a slow and understanding smile. "Some people won't have it that he's handsome, but I think he's much more than that ... almost frighteningly handsome. The devil's half-brother, I once heard him called. Think of having him at your elbow for a week, supporting you, advising you! For my sake he'll do that."

"No," Janie repeated—but it was a weaker "No" this time. "I couldn't."

CHAPTER III

MAX VELDON frowned as a tap came at his door. He was the occupant of a very large suite in a very impressive London hotel, and when the interruption came he was at his desk, and had just put down the telephone receiver.

"Come in," he snapped. He had a quiet voice —a deadly quiet voice—and underlying it was a continuous note of impatience. It also had a very faint Austrian accent.

A liveried hotel porter stood aside for Janie to enter. She had lost herself in the maze of thickly-carpeted corridors once she left the lift behind her, and the porter had come to her rescue. He looked at her pityingly when he saw the way in which the musician regarded her as he stood up reluctantly to greet her.

"Sit down." He thrust a chair towards her. It was a spindly-legged chair covered in satin damask, and Janie sat down on the edge of it. The man resumed his seat at the desk. "You are Miss Dallas?" he said. "Miss Jane Dallas?" His inscrutable dark eyes made her feel cold and unacceptable as they roved over her. "I've just been talking to Miss Brandt on the telephone, and I'll confess I don't quite understand why she is taking such a risk. Such an appalling risk!" His voice hardened, his eyes grew bleak and cold as arrow-heads. "Have you anything to do with it, or is this notion all hers?"

"It certainly isn't mine." Janie found it impossible to prevent her voice from trembling, but part of the unsteadiness was due to indignation on her part. "You surely don't imagine that I thought of such a dangerous piece of deception? For one thing, I don't really look in the least like Miss Brandt ——"

"You look sufficiently like her to deceive some people if they haven't already met you," he cut her short brusquely. "Or Miss Brandt, of course! Anyone who knows Miss Brandt as I do wouldn't be deceived for a moment."

"No, of course not," she agreed, moistening her lips. "But Miss Brandt thought . . . when I've had my hair re-styled, and I'm wearing different clothes. . . ."

"You most certainly will have to wear different clothes," he agreed, and the glance of contempt he cast at her neat grey suit and modest accessories made something inside her feel as if it was curling up after the assault of a whiplash. "Very different clothes!"

She bit her lip.

"I've never had occasion to wear anything but

very simple clothes, Mr. Veldon," she told him. "Quite apart from the fact that I've never had the money to buy anything but simple clothes."

"Quite," he agreed coldly. "You do, in fact, belong to an entirely different world from the one which contains Miss Brandt," and he rose and started pacing about the room in his superbly tailored suit; a slim live-wire of a man with a debonair touch lent to his appearance by the flower in his buttonhole and his carelessly flowing tie, but with nothing else that was debonair about him.

There was a kind of fluid grace to his movements which did nothing to detract from the impression of primitiveness which he exuded . . . and Janie knew why, when he took his place on a rostrum and lifted his baton, the women in the audience watched him with an almost suffocating sensation of excitement—as she had done once. For he was like an elegant caged tiger with music in his blood, and at a distance one didn't see the bleakness in his eyes . . . the criticism. One only knew that his eyes must be dark, and that darkness predominated where he was concerned.

Dark eyes, dark hair, an impeccable set of faultless dark tails, with a white tie highlighting his square dark chin.

Exciting under the lights, with the orchestra swelling into a crescendo . . . but forbidding in a hotel room!

"You work for Miss Brandt's father?" he asked, his tone as remote as a falling star.

"Yes," she answered.

"He is, I believe, an antique dealer?"

Janie supposed that that could be one description of old Hermann Brandt's disgracefully cluttered junk shop in a corner of London where antiques were not much sought after, and nodded her head.

"In that case you probably know a lot about antiques, but nothing about music?"

"On the contrary," she replied, "I know practically nothing about antiques, but I do love music."

"So?" he said, and sent her a long and curious glance. "A lot of people love music, but their knowledge of it is grossly limited."

"Try me," she invited, when he had seated himself again at his desk. "Put me through a sort of catechism, and I'll answer you to the best of my ability."

"Then what do you know of Brahms?" he asked.

She gave him a concise but correct history of the life of Brahms.

"Beethoven?"

She sketched the life of Beethoven briefly but almost poignantly. His eyebrows ascended.

"You have mugged all this up for my benefit?" he asked.

"Oh, no," she assured him. "That wasn't necessary, because my father was Stephen Dallas, and he wrote a book called *The Great Ones*. It wasn't, unfortunately, a great success, but it was a part of my reading when I was still not much more than a child."

"I know the book," he told her. "As a matter of fact, I've got it in my library." He stared hard at her. "So you're the daughter of Stephen Dallas, and he no doubt passed on to you his ability to appreciate music. Is that why you say you love it?"

"I suppose so."

His expression grew dry again.

"Don't tell me that, through the benignity of an understanding Providence, you also sing like the Brandt?"

"No, I don't sing at all," she answered quietly. "And I don't suppose many women have a voice like hers."

"You are quite right," he agreed, with brusque finality. "Not one in a million." He passed her a box of cigarettes, and she waited for him to light one for her. His gold lighter had a severity which matched his personality, but it also had his initials in diamonds on one side of it, and she wondered whether it was the gift of a fan. "The trouble with Vanessa is that she works too hard, and becomes caught up by too many enthusiasms, with the result that she has acquired what is known as a tired throat. Is it because you are sorry for her that you wish to help her, or because she is paying you well?"

"She is not paying me at all," Janie said curtly.

He smiled unpleasantly.

"And the gift of an entirely new outfit of clothes, visits to beauty parlours, etc., is nothing? Means nothing? You couldn't possibly be tempted by trifles like those?"

This time it was she who looked hard at him with her steady grey eyes.

"No," she said.

He smiled disbelievingly.

"Not even the thought of a week in a luxury hotel? The sheer glamour attached to such an opportunity! Nothing like that has anything to do with your decision to play a part?—and a very difficult part at that! For Vanessa has personality as well as looks, and you will be required to put over Vanessa as she is at her best. Did you realize that?"

"Yes. And I am not attracted by glamour, or anything you have mentioned."

"Then what?" He was leaning towards her, his own cigarette smouldering between his fingers, his eyes alive and bright with sudden curiosity. "What, Miss Dallas?"

She found herself faltering, and looking away

from him. He had very long eyelashes—ridiculously long for a man—and they fluttered as he talked. She kept seeing him as he was when he stood on the rostrum, baton in hand . . . the very essence of strange, compelling masculine charm. Masculine mystery.

"I . . . don't think I quite know," she answered at last.

He looked intensely cynical all at once.

"Then we'll accept simply that it's the glamour," he said. "I never thought for one moment that it was anything else." He crushed out his cigarette in the ashtray, and pushed back his chair to cut short the interview. "I've given my word to Miss Brandt, whom I admire tremendously, that I'll see this thing through . . . although my every instinct warns me that it's crazy. She's risking everything she's worked for by allowing you to impersonate her even for a day. You look like her, you may be able to act like her, but I doubt it."

"And if you're wrong, Mr. Veldon?" she asked, feeling herself stiffen as if something had put her on her mettle, and not merely was it vital to her own future interests to prove him wrong, but it was curiously and intensely vital.

"Then I'll probably dislike you a little less than I do at this moment," he returned contemptuously, treating her to a look of absolute dislike. "Now

you'd better run along and see my secretary. She
has a list of appointments she has made for you
—all under cover of the strictest secrecy, of
course!" dryly—"and I hope you'll be ready to fly
with me to New York in forty-eight hours."

CHAPTER IV

It was a whirlwind forty-eight hours for Janie.
Before they expired the curl had been taken out of
her hair, and it was bound sleekly and smoothly
about her head, her complexion was several
degrees fairer, and for the first time in her life she
wore eye make-up.

The effect was to deepen the colour of her eyes,
so that in certain lights, and under certain con-
ditions, they could have been blue instead of grey.
And as Vanessa Brandt had a weakness for veiling,
even with cocktail hats, this was a help, too.

Her clothes were chosen for her in a great hurry
by Max Veldon's secretary. She managed to get
certain people to work overtime, so that various
alterations were carried out with the minimum loss
of time; and certain dresses selected from Vanessa's own wardrobe had the essential alterations to
them carried out quickly.

Vanessa was a shade taller than Janie, and her
figure just a little fuller. But by the time the dresses
were altered no one would have guessed that they
hadn't, in the first place, been created for Janie.
An evening gown in gold brocade, suitable for very
grand occasions, took her breath away completely.

She had never dreamed that she would ever wear a gold brocade evening gown.

Miss Calendar, Max Veldon's secretary, was an alert little woman of uncertain age who had been with him for years. He had, also, one or two other secretaries, but these were men, responsible for stage-managing and publicizing him wherever he went, and only one of them accompanied him to New York.

He was a handsome, dark-eyed young Austrian —a half-brother to Max. His mother had been a baroness in her own right, and the title had devolved upon Rudi, who did not, however, use it.

"In Austria we bury our titles these days," he told Janie, when he met her for the first time at the airport. Miss Calendar introduced them a trifle agitatedly, and in the midst of her agitation she called him "Baron."

He held up a finger to her.

"Tut, tut, Miss Calendar, what a lapse! Whoever heard of a baron without any money? And, apart from the occasions when Max is generous, I have none!"

His eyes, black and audacious, smiled into Janie's. They had an extraordinary lustre that lent them the appearance of sparkling black velvet, and every feature of his face was fascinatingly regular. But, despite hair with a kink in it, and teeth like blanched almonds—and long and shapely fingers that pressed a little too warmly when they closed over a woman's hand—Janie had an instinctive urge not to trust him too far.

Or, at any rate, not to be beguiled by him.

"You are quite enchanting," he told her, when they sat together in the aircraft. His half-brother and Miss Calendar occupied the seat across the aisle, and were both deep in the perusal of a batch of correspondence. "Only a fool would be deceived into thinking you were Vanessa."

She looked at him in a startled fashion.

"But that means I'm going to let her down——!"

"Don't worry," he said soothingly, resting a hand over hers where they were tightly, and somewhat convulsively, clasped in her lap. "I say that because I know her well, and to me she no longer has—what shall we call it? Freshness? She has the charm of sophistication, but you have the charm of the early morning. Otherwise you are much alike."

"Thank you," Janie said, a faint note of asperity, instead of appreciation, in her voice. "I feel considerably relieved."

He laughed.

"You should be flattered, and under normal circumstances I've no doubt you would be. For what can be more delightful than the early morning? But I realize you have a part to play, and the thought of it must be weighing on you. But don't worry too much, for I will support you . . . I will make everything as easy as it can possibly be made for you."

Janie regarded him thoughtfully, endeavouring to sum him up. Deep down inside her anxiety started to grow because she felt that in a sense he had her in the hollow of his hand.

"I suppose," she said slowly, "that Mr. Veldon had to let you into Miss Brandt's secret. If you're his brother, and you know her very well, too. . . ."

"I don't know her quite as well as Max," he confessed, a smile which she didn't like at all on his lips, and a sleepy glitter in his eyes as he slid them across the aisle at his brother. "But I do know her . . . reasonably well. And of course I had to be in on this, otherwise I could have given the whole show away before it actually became a show at all, couldn't I?"

"You mean that if Mr. Veldon hadn't consented to your accompanying us you could—would have given away something that has to be kept secret?"

He shook his head.

"No, little one, I wouldn't have done that, because Max would cut me off with a penny if I let him down like that. But I'm not at all sure I would have been permitted to accompany him, as you phrase it, if I hadn't accidentally blundered on this secret you're going to find it a little hard to guard sometimes . . . if you're not perpetually alert and a consummate actress!'"

Her grey eyes grew large and round with anxiety as she gazed at him.

"I've no reason at all to believe that I'm even a remotely good actress, Baron Eisler," she told him. "But because I've got to be, there isn't any doubt that I'll be perpetually alert."

"Of course." He gave her hand another pat, and smiled at her encouragingly—and with a warmth that should have banished all mistrust. "And you can depend upon it that I'll help you, as I've said —in every possible way that I can help you. If only you'll do one thing."

"And what is that?" she asked uneasily.

"Call me Rudi, and forget all that nonsense about Baron Eisler. I'd much rather be Rudi to you."

When they arrived in New York Janie came close to pure panic. Max was looking distinctly grim, and he had hardly addressed a word to her during the flight. Every time she accidentally met his eyes their coldness and disapproval made her feel as if she herself was cold inside, and she had a wild urge to back out long before she said farewell to the interior of the aircraft.

Max must have sensed this, for when he helped her into the sleek and glistening private car that had been sent to meet them at the airport he gripped her arm hard. It was a distinctly cruel grip.

"Panic now, and everything's lost," he said. "And if you fail Vanessa I'll never forgive you!"

The unfeeling threat in his voice was like an icy douche that brought her up gasping protestingly but determined never to merit such another warning.

"I won't fail her," she said in a low tone.

"Better not," he emphasized, and released her arm.

Miss Calendar—who had consistently addressed her as "Miss Brandt" from the moment they left London—saw her effusively on to the back seat of the car, and an enormous bouquet of flowers was then placed in her lap. It was the second bouquet she had received in a matter of hours, for the stewardess had brought her a mass of red roses with a fulsome card attached—*"From one of your most ardent admirers"*—as soon as she set foot in the aircraft that had just brought her, for the first time, across the Atlantic.

With the stewardess looking on and beaming at her and admiring her silvery-beige outfit, and the mink coat without which Vanessa had insisted a top-line singer of her quality never travelled—"If you carry this thing through successfully I'll give it to you before we part!" she had promised, when Janie went to say goodbye to her in the nursing-

home—she had stammered and looked confused
and practically denied that such a passionate tribute could be for her.

Until Miss Calendar swept to her rescue and
requested the stewardess to place the roses in water
until Miss Brandt reached New York. Janie had
sent her a grateful look—which she was quite sure
Max Veldon intercepted, because his expression
had taken on an even grimmer look—and the second time she received flowers she was careful not
to betray any surprise.

"For me?" she inquired, sweetly and languidly,
and the uniformed chauffeur who had bent to tuck
a light rug over her knees answered at once. His
eyes expressed admiration for the slight, golden-
headed figure as he did so.

"With Mr. Winterton's compliments, Miss
Brandt."

Janie merely smiled at him, as if she was touched
but exhausted.

She didn't need the rug, for the airport was
heating up—a long, hot June day stretched ahead
of her, which she was to find really exhausting before it reached its close—and she didn't need to
pretend that she had scarcely slept a wink all night,
for the slight pallor of her face proclaimed it. In
a way it was a good thing, for no one was likely to
attribute her lethargy to a petrified feeling due to
the novelty of a first flight, and a secret terror that,

sooner or later, she must give herself away. People were much more likely to assume that she was bored by too much travelling, and was a poor traveller in any case.

Rudi sat beside her in the car, and Max Veldon was stiff and unco-operative on her other side. Miss Calendar chatted blithely in the seat beside the chauffeur.

When they drew up outside the great hotel where a suite had been reserved for Janie, the morning—her first New York morning—was really brilliant. But she stumbled awkwardly from the car, and was led away to the lift. She thought of it afterwards as an ornamental cage that wafted her away from prying eyes.

For only Miss Calendar accompanied her into the suite, and she went round opening all the windows that were not already opened, and adjusting the sun-blinds so that not one single shaft of brazen sunshine penetrated to the rooms. They were high above the street, and they were literally banked with flowers.

Janie made out baskets of carnations and cascades of gardenias and roses, all so pale that they were like flowery ghosts in the gloom. Abraham Winterton had scrawled his tribute on an enormous gilt-edged card that was set up on the dressing-table, where she couldn't possibly miss it.

"Welcome to one of the loveliest of singers! Tonight I shall give myself the happiness of seeing you. I am giving a party for you in my flat, and you mustn't disappoint me by being too tired for it."

Janie felt herself grow weak and rather faint. The scent of the massed flowers was almost overpowering, and the hint of command in that flowery handwriting appalled her. She realized that Abraham Winterton wouldn't be merely disappointed if she failed to attend his party—*her* party!—but mortally offended.

Miss Calendar came across to her and relieved her of her gloves and handbag.

"Get out of your things and into a cool wrap and lie down," she suggested. "And you'll feel much better after a good sleep. And if you'd like me to split up this florist's shop and put some of it outside in the corridor I'll do so."

"Please," Janie gasped. "I think I must have developed an allergy to flowers."

Miss Calendar smiled sympathetically. Janie had already decided that she was likely to prove her one real friend and supporter during the difficult days that lay ahead.

"If you have, you'd better conquer it," she advised. "Because Abraham Winterton is a rich man, and so are most of his friends."

When Janie awoke she was still in the room, and water was running into the bath in the adjoining bathroom. To the perfume of the flowers was added the rich aroma of costly bath essence, and Miss Calendar was draping a slim sheath of white satin over the back of a chair.

"There's the dress you're going to wear this evening," she said, "and everything's ready for you. I've unpacked and put out all your make-up things, and you've only to step into your bath and then I'll do the rest."

"But you're not a personal maid," Janie objected.

Miss Calendar shrugged.

"We thought it best not to put too much of a strain on Miss Brandt's personal maid by bringing her with us," she explained. "The girl is French, and a trifle voluble, and we were not altogether sure we could trust her. But I've done most things in my life, and looking after you won't wear me out."

"But won't Mr. Veldon miss you——?" Janie began.

"Naturally, I'm acting under Mr. Veldon's instructions," Miss Calendar informed her with a faint lift of her eyebrows.

Of course! Janie sank back on her bed again, limply. Mr. Veldon's instructions! ... Mr. Veldon was ruthless, and he would instruct and organize and drive her until she scarcely knew what she was doing, or why she was doing it. As she lay there on the bed she certainly had no clear idea why she was putting herself through this ordeal and impersonating Vanessa Brandt, and the knowledge that she couldn't carry through such an impersonation overwhelmed her all at once. She said fearfully:

"Do I have to go to that party tonight? Couldn't an excuse be made for me? After all, Mr. Winterton can't expect me to be very fresh...."

"Singers are always fresh," Miss Calendar told her, looking at her expressionlessly. "They have to be."

"Of course."

Janie struggled off the bed. There came a knock at the outer door of the sitting-room, and Miss Calendar answered it and came back with a cellophane carton of golden roses in her hand. She handed them to Janie.

"From the Baron von Eisler," she said, her face still expressionless. "You can't possibly wear them, because Mr. Winterton has sent you orchids, but I should thank the Baron very nicely for them when you see him. He's another one we can't trust, and these people have to be handled rather carefully sometimes."

CHAPTER V

MR. WINTERTON turned out to be quite unlike Janie's preconceived idea of the sort of man he would prove to be. She had imagined a slightly bloated impresario type, with wealth leering at her every time he smiled, and opportunity beckoning to her when he lifted his plump fingers.

But Abraham Winterton—although he was certainly a very wealthy man—was also a very charming one. He was tall and spare and beautifully dressed, his tailor obviously a man who practised restraint, and his shirtmaker and shoemaker and so forth men with similar ideas. He had greying hair and a whimsical smile, and the diamonds in his shirt-cuffs were opulent without being vulgar.

Janie felt both her hands caught by him and taken into a firm clasp, and he said as he eyed her with admiration:

"It is an astonishing thing to me that you and I have never met before . . . not as we are meeting now. I have admired you for years, and listening to your voice has given me the greatest pleasure, yet now that we meet at last I can scarcely believe that someone hasn't played a trick." Janie raised startled eyes to his face. "You are so very much younger than I had supposed you would be. I mean," gallantly, "when you were at the very commencement of your career you could hardly have looked more like a schoolgirl than you do now that you have arrived at the very peak of it!"

Janie blushed, and wondered what she could find to say to that.

Winterton made it unnecessary for her to say anything.

"I see that you are wearing my orchids." He smiled quizzically. "I was afraid that you might be tired of them . . . but orchids are, after all, such very perfect flowers, just as you, Miss Brandt, are such a perfect young woman," and he bowed over her hands and even kissed them lightly.

His flat was so sumptuous that Janie wanted to cast glances round her and admire everything openly. She wondered what Hermann Brandt would think of the piano that occupied an entire corner of the huge room into which they were first shown, and the beautiful bronze of Beethoven that stood on a pedestal in a kind of alcove. Brandt worshipped at the shrine of Beethoven, and the bronze would have riveted his attention at once. And the hangings falling from ceiling to floor before the wide open windows were of golden mesh, while the carpet was a sea of gold.

Abraham Winterton took her by the hand and

introduced her to the rest of his guests—and there were so many of them that Janie was appalled. So many people who had to be deceived, and who might possibly have seen her—or rather, Vanessa! —somewhere before. In an opera house where her heavy make-up would have concealed the true Vanessa, in her own dressing-room, perhaps—and Janie hoped fervently that Vanessa never discarded her make-up before the last person who wanted to be presented to her found his or her way round to the back of the theatre. Or, very likely, in a restaurant, or a hotel foyer.

So she was immensely relieved when no one appeared to stare at her rather harder than they should, and the eager voices that addressed her had nothing more alarming to say to her than:

"I remember when I heard you sing in Milan ... at La Scala. It was wonderful, and I shall never forget what an enchanting Mimi you made. So many Mimis are fat, even if their voices are marvellous ... but you were perfect! And in Vienna, in *Madam Butterfly* ... how did you manage to look so completely Oriental, when you are so golden?"

"Like a golden rose," Rudi murmured in her ear, having managed to insinuate himself in a space just behind her. "That was why I sent you golden roses!"

Janie looked round at him, and found his dark

lustrous eyes gazing down at her with an openly caressing look in them. But behind the caressing look was one that was faintly reproachful.

"You are not wearing them," he murmured.

Abraham Winterton was forced to devote some of his attention to other of his guests, and Janie was glad of an opportunity to sink back into temporary obscurity beside Rudi, and to have him extricate her from the crush and guide her out on to a balcony beyond a swaying waterfall of golden mesh.

"But you did like them, didn't you?" he asked, looking at her curiously as they stood together with the roar of New York far below them, and the stars in a deeply purple night sky not very far removed from them, or so it seemed.

"Of course," she answered, a trifle breathlessly —for she had only just survived the biggest ordeal of her life.

"And I understand perfectly why you couldn't wear them." His gaze had dropped sardonically to the orchids attached to her shoulder. "If you were you, and not Vanessa—and Vanessa is always out to make more and more money; so much you must understand—you would have worn them for me tonight, wouldn't you, *liebling?*"

The unfamiliar German endearment startled her.

"I don't know," she answered.

He smiled at her in the star-pricked, suffocatingly hot dark, and she had never known white teeth flash as his flashed.

"But of course you would, lovely one. Already I admire you so much, and you must be aware of it——"

The golden mesh parted behind them, and a shadow stood there close to them. Max Veldon said coldly to Janie:

"This party will go on for hours, and you had better fortify yourself. Come with me to the buffet and I'll see that you get something to eat as well as drink." He glanced at his brother as if he didn't exist. "Besides, it's a bad thing to disappear when you are the star guest!"

Rudi leant against the parapet and smiled indolently. In his white tie and tails he was almost shatteringly handsome.

"So the curtain has gone up, dear brother," he said, "and no doubt you are consumed with anxiety? But don't worry! Our little Miss Dallas here has already done remarkably well . . . she had Winterton practically eating out of her hand, he was so charmed with her. I doubt whether the real Vanessa would have won that compliment about looking like a schoolgirl!"

Veldon ignored him, although his eyes were gimlet-hard as he gazed at him for a moment.

"Will you come this way, Miss Brandt?"

"I prefer to think of her as Jane," Rudi murmured. "It's such a soft little name."

When they were well away from the balcony Veldon looked down at Janie.

"You do realize that you are not here for your own amusement, don't you, Miss Dallas?" he asked. She had the feeling that he was furiously angry with her because he had to address her by her own name. "If my brother wants to flirt with you you must discourage him at all costs. *At all costs*, do you understand?" He took her by the arm, and once more his fingers bruised her flesh. "Vanessa is above that sort of thing, and you must be, too! When this week is over, and you are a free agent, you may do as you please . . . if Rudi still thinks of you then as a source of entertainment!"

"Mr. Veldon!" she gasped. Then her face flushed painfully. "I think you meant that to be as beastly as it sounds," she said.

"I did," he admitted. "And if you are so simple that you can be deceived by a few outrageous compliments and a handful of yellow roses——"

"So you know about the roses," she remarked quietly.

"Of course. And make no mistake, whatever happens to you during the next few days—while you are here in New York!—I shall know about that, too. Vanessa's interests are important to me, and you will be under constant observation. So don't imagine you can sit back and enjoy yourself as if this was a holiday you haven't earned. You can enjoy yourself on the strength of my personal cheque for one thousand pounds when—and if— you carry this thing through for Miss Brandt, and land her a contract."

She flushed still more painfully.

"I wouldn't touch your money, Mr. Veldon," she told him.

He shrugged. He piloted her into a room where a great horseshoe table which practically ringed it was laden with everything from caviare to fresh salmon that had been leaping about in a Scottish river only a matter of hours before, champagne and vodka, and asked her what she would like.

"Nothing," she answered, feeling as if she would choke.

The host swooped upon them and apologized profusely for deserting the side of his principal guest, and himself put a glass of champagne into Janie's hand. If he wondered why her colour was a trifle high he naturally made no comment.

"I'm hoping very much that before the evening is out I can persuade you to sing for us, Miss Brandt," he said, and the champagne glass nearly fell from her hand. But a smooth voice with a faint but attractive accent came to her rescue.

"I'm afraid you'll have to excuse Miss Brandt tonight, Mr. Winterton," Max Veldon said. "She had a slight but unfortunate accident when leaving the plane this morning, and her ankle was slightly twisted. She was complaining to me just now that it hurts her a little... which means that it hurts her a great deal! I was about to suggest that you could be induced to excuse her, and that she retires early...."

"But of course, Miss Brandt!" Abraham Winterton exclaimed with instant sympathy. "My dear young lady," he added swiftly, understanding perfectly now why she had looked agitated when he interrupted her conversation with the famous conductor, "you should have told me of this at once! You shouldn't have attempted to come here tonight . . . you should have telephoned——!"

Janie felt faint with the relief that swirled over her.

"It isn't anything at all serious," she tried to reassure the concerned impresario. "In fact, it isn't really anything at all."

"Of course, of course," he said, patting her hand and sounding very fatherly—although there was nothing fatherly about the admiration for her that still lingered in his eyes. "I understand perfectly, and you are merely trying to be brave because you don't wish to spoil my party, or me to be disappointed. But I assure you most seriously that I shall be very upset if you don't go back to your hotel at once and rest that foot."

An anxious glance at it could detect no swelling, but her colour had faded and she did look pale— with the excess of her relief, had he but known it —as Max Veldon drew her hand through his arm and forced her to lean on him.

"Take her back to the hotel at once, Veldon," Winterton said urgently. "If I could leave my guests I'd take her back myself, but it isn't possible." He cast rather an abstracted glance at his guests. "But unless I hear in the morning that the ankle is better I shall send my own doctor to have a look at it." He smiled at Janie, and his smile was singularly reassuring to her just then. "Don't think that because we've brought you all the way to New York we're going to wear you out now that you are here! If necessary—and I understand you've recently concluded a most exhausting tour —I'll arrange for you to have an absolutely peaceful time while you're here, and a complete rest. As a matter of fact——"

But Veldon assured him that anything like that would be quite unnecessary, and Miss Brandt would be quite herself in the morning. Taking her cue from him, Janie echoed that she would be quite all right in the morning, and Winterton kissed her hand as delicately and tenderly as if it was a particularly fragile flower and permitted her to escape without making her farewells to anyone save himself.

In the car which took them back to the hotel Janie lay back and closed her eyes, and Veldon glanced at her rather thoughtfully. She looked like someone who was drained of initiative, or even the power to think, and abruptly he remarked that she might do worse than suffer a genuine sprained ankle.

Janie opened her eyes and fixed them upon him curiously, and very wearily.

"You mean," she inquired, with a certain amount of unusual dryness in her voice, "that you might be able to arrange it?"

He studied her with inscrutable dark eyes over the glowing tip of his cigarette, and a sudden movement of the car sent her up against his shoulder. She withdrew from his quickly as if the contact was most unpleasant.

"If a sprained ankle would simplify matters for you—and Vanessa!—it might be worth while arranging," he murmured. "But how shall we arrange it?" His dark eyes mocked her harshly. "Shall I throw you out of the car window, or grease the stairs for you to slip upon?" His white teeth gleamed cruelly in the gloom of the interior of the car. "Or shall I think up some other means?"

She regarded him as if something about him fascinated her all at once.

"You might be capable of something of the sort," she answered, "but at least you saved me half an hour ago. I'm grateful to you, Mr. Veldon."

"You needn't be," he answered curtly. "That was to save Vanessa, not you!"

CHAPTER VI

Miss Calendar, when she heard about the sprained ankle, was concerned.

"But what if Mr. Winterton sends his doctor here to examine Miss Dallas's ankle?" she said, when Veldon paid a visit to the suite early the following morning.

"He won't," Veldon answered. "And if he did it wouldn't greatly matter. We could say the swelling had gone down overnight."

Janie, who had just emerged from her bath, and was combing her hair in the bedroom, heard them talking, and was not in the least surprised when the door was thrust open without ceremony and Veldon himself stood there looking at her. She saw his eyebrows shoot upwards in mild surprise.

"Oh, so you're up," he remarked, as if he had expected to find her still in bed. "Vanessa wouldn't have even contemplated rising for another hour or so."

"I'm accustomed to early rising," she told him, the comb suspended in mid-air.

He moved leisurely across the room until he stood beside her at the dressing-table. She was wearing a pale rose-coloured satin dressing-gown,

and she looked all rose and gold and creamy whiteness flushed from the warmth of her bath. She wore
no make-up, and the tendrils of her hair were curling tightly from the moisture of the bathroom, and
his eye fastened on one of them.

"I hope you won't think me unreasonable if I
ask whether this visit is a very important one?" she
said slowly, lowering the comb to the dressing-
table. She stood with her hands straight down at her
sides. "Or a very necessary one at such an hour?"

"Why?" he asked, as if he was curious. "I mean,
why do you wish to know?"

"Because I don't encourage visits from members of the opposite sex to my bedroom at any time
during the twenty-four hours, and I particularly
object when they don't even knock at the door."

His head went up, and then he smiled curiously.

"To me it doesn't greatly matter what your prac-
tice is, since you are not Miss Dallas but Miss
Brandt."

"Then, in the name of Miss Brandt, and not
Miss Dallas, and because I feel sure that she, too,
occasionally prefers not to be intruded upon—I
must ask you to return to the sitting-room and
allow me to get dressed."

The smile died slowly out of his eyes, and his
lips twisted queerly.

"Meaning that Miss Brandt has no objection to
being intruded upon if she is in the mood for it?"

"Possibly."

"While you—the pretty little assistant in an antique shop!—have prudish notions, owing to the way in which you were brought up?"

"You can attribute it to my upbringing if you like."

He turned away, and she watched him stride back to the door of the sitting-room. He said curtly:

"I'll wait for you in the sitting-room. There are one or two things I want to talk to you about."

She was wearing a corn-silk suit when she joined him, and her hair was a corn-silk cloud about her shoulders. He frowned.

"Vanessa always wears her hair in that kind of little bun arrangement."

"Even Vanessa might adopt new fashions," she replied. "And an elaborate hair-style is too much to attempt at this hour of the morning."

"But it makes you look much too young, worn like that." Then a curious expression crossed his face, and he shrugged his shoulders. "However, you seem to have made a tremendous impression on our friend Winterton, and the one thing about you that appears to have struck him is your youth ... or your semblance of youth!" He was watching her very closely as he continued: "Vanessa is twenty-six, and she has lived every moment of the last ten of them to the full, with the result that she sometimes looks older than her twenty-six years. However, she is not here, and you are . . . and it is to you we have to look for that contract for Vanessa. So you can wear your hair in a pony-tail if you wish!"

She refused to smile, or appear even mildly amused.

"Winterton—or rather, one of his secretaries—has already put through a couple of calls to this hotel this morning," Veldon informed her, "and more flowers are on their way. Winterton also wishes you to lunch with him—that is, if you are fit enough, and we've assured him that you are," —dryly—"and it's to be a completly *tête-à-tête* affair in his flat. No one else is invited."

She immediately looked alarmed.

"Oh, but——"

He held up one of his slim and shapely hands— that looked extra slim and shapely by contrast with the whiteness of his cuff.

"There is no need for you to look as if you have been invited into the wolves' parlour, for Winterton is a very courtly person, and very charming to members of your sex. He will not eat you," with faint contempt. "But he may make a little light love to you, so don't be too stand-offish, or repel him with anything in the nature of violence. Remember that it is Vanessa's interests you have at heart!"

"And Vanessa would not repel him if he made love to her?"

For the first time she thought the expression on his face was a little wry.

"Shall we say she would not go out of her way to damage her own prospects, if those prospects were sufficiently good," he replied, and lighted himself a cigarette with a good deal of quiet deliberation.

"I see," Janie said.

He looked across the flower-filled room at her, through the thin haze of smoke which had started to float between them.

"And what if he asks questions? Searching questions?" Janie inquired. "How do I answer them?"

"To the best of your ability," Veldon ordered her. "And with discretion. The one thing you must not forget is that you are doing this for Vanessa."

"I'm scarcely likely to do that," Janie remarked with acute dryness.

He watched her for a moment, provided her with a fleeting impression that he was about to say something else, and then rose. He said, in the businesslike tone of an employer directing his personal assistant's movements for the day:

"After lunch you will come back here and rest, and this evening you will attend a concert at which I will conduct the orchestra. It is a charitable affair to raise funds for refugees, and the most important personage likely to be there is the Princess Olga Oranovski. She is a Russian who married an extremely wealthy American, but for occasions like this she makes use of her former title. You know how the Americans love titles, in spite of their democratic pretensions, and her presence alone will ensure a large audience."

"So long as I'm not asked to sing," Janie returned, "I shall enjoy watching you conduct."

He replied arrogantly:

"You should. And you most certainly will not be asked to sing."

But before she could look forward to any possibility of relaxing at a concert—and although she had said so demurely, "I shall enjoy watching you conduct," Janie was actually thrilled by the prospect of once more being permitted to do so, dislike the man behind the conductor though she did very thoroughly by this time—she had yet to survive the ordeal of having a *tête-à-tête* lunch with Abraham Winterton, and the girl who was impersonating Vanessa Brandt could not look forward to that.

She knew that it wouldn't be possible for her to be off her guard for one moment, and one single error of speech might precipitate an intolerable situation. So—although she had found Abraham Winterton charming and courtly enough, and she wasn't very badly frightened by the thought that he might make a little light love to her (After all,

what was a little light love, when you were in
danger of being exposed as a fraud?)—Janie
dressed with a great deal of trepidation and inner
foreboding for the lunch, and was only just ready
to be escorted out to the car that had been sent for
her when it arrived and Miss Calendar started
reiterating various warnings, and giving her large
quantities of advice.

"Whatever you do, don't allow yourself to be
drawn on the subject of your early days," Miss
Calendar cautioned her. "And remember that
you've travelled extensively. So I wouldn't discuss
travel, if I were you!"

On the way down in the lift Rudi managed to
insinuate himself into the space behind her, and
she heard him murmur ironically into her ear:

"Good hunting! Don't let the side down, and
bring back the contract for Vanessa. Then we can
start enjoying ourselves!"

She had no confused notions on the subject of
what Rudi von Eisler meant by that.

Abraham Winterton was even more charming
when he received her in the vast entrance hall of
his palatial flat. He was full of concern for her
ankle, and full of self-reproach because he had
wanted to see her again so badly that he couldn't
allow her to rest and recover herself as she should
have done.

"You've just completed an exhausting tour, and

now you should rest," he said. "But people like myself will not let you rest! We cannot see and hear
enough of you, and that is the truth!'"

He led her out on to a kind of roof-garden, where
they sipped aperitifs before lunch actually began.
Janie had changed into an enchanting and very
smart outfit of lilac silk with white accessories, and
amongst the pot plants and the umbrellas and the
spraying fountains she looked as delicate as a piece
of porcelain. Not perhaps as *soignée* and sophisti-
cated as Vanessa would have done on such an
occasion—and with so much at stake!—but with
a cameo perfection about her, and touchingly
young. A tribute to the art of make-up, the man
could suppose, but a very great tribute at that.

"You are so much more beautiful than I had
ever dreamed," he told her, touching her hand
caressingly when he put her glass into it. "Not
beautiful in a hard and classical sense, as some of
your photographs have suggested, but with a kind
of gossamer beauty." He smiled a little selfconsciously, and in spite of the touches of white in
his hair, and the lines at the corners of his eyes and
mouth—lines of experience and knowledge, she
realized—there was something boyish about his appearance in the broad daylight. "You must forgive me if I try to say things which trip me up,
but I haven't any Latin blood in my veins, and
pretty speeches don't come easily. But I've admired

you for a very long time—which seems impossible, when I merely look at you!—and now I've made the discovery that the reality is infinitely more attractive than the woman I've simply dreamed about!"

Janie swallowed.

"I'm very flattered, Mr. Winterton, that you have . . . dreamed about me!"

He smiled, and this time he made no pretence about capturing her hand.

"The quality of your voice enchants my ear, and therefore you had to enchant me, too. It was as inevitable as that."

"You—you believe in inevitability, Mr. Winterton?" she asked, for something to say.

"Of course," he replied. "And the odd thing is I'm not just putting myself out to make flattering speeches to you, because I hope to persuade you to accept a part that I believe was created for you in a musical show I am putting on, but as a woman you interest me . . . far, far more than as a singer."

Did this, she wonder, come into the category of light love-making, or was the earnestness she sensed behind his words an indication that his mood was not a light one? At that particular moment, anyway!

She felt vaguely, queerly alarmed.

"Miss Brandt . . . or may I call you Vanessa?" he pleaded.

"Of course," she answered.

"Then, Vanessa—enchanting Vanessa!—I'm a lonely man at heart, a confirmed bachelor—or so most people believe!—who gets occasionally bored by women, because he sees too much of them. But you are so utterly unlike anyone I've ever met before, that I——"

He took a hurried gulp at his own drink, and then offered to refill hers. She shook her head.

"No, thank you. I hardly drink at all."

"You are amazing," he said. "Unless, of course, you are on some sort of a diet. . . ? Medical advice, perhaps?"

"No, nothing like that. I just don't like it."

"Amazing," he repeated. "And when I think of all the champagne suppers given in your honour, the wearisome lunches you are forced to attend. ... ."

He waited, and she did what Vanessa would have done in the circumstances, smiled at him under her long and curving eyelashes and assured him that she had looked forward very much to this lunch today. She had even counted the hours before she left London—and she hoped that the flagrant untruth would be forgiven her!—because the thought of meeting him, the great Abraham Winterton, was as exciting as anything she had ever looked forward to.

Winterton beamed at her, and seemed quite delighted by her confession.

"Dear lady!" he exclaimed, and captured her hand again and kissed it several times. "Dear, delightful young woman! And if you only knew how *I* have looked forward to having you as my guest!"

The lunch was a delicious one for such a hot day, and Janie was excused taking more than a sip of champagne—and it was highly important, she realized, that she should keep all her wits about her—because it didn't appeal to her. Winterton asked her quite a number of questions about her past life and background, and because she had been provided with most of the answers she was able to deal with them. There were one or two, however, that very nearly defeated her, and but for a wrongful interpretation which her host placed on her disinclination to talk about certain aspects and phases of her life, she might have given herself away at that very first lunch she had alone with the great man.

As it was, her hesitation brought a smile, and he said as if he was actually rather pleased:

"I can tell you do not care to dwell upon all your many triumphs, and that is a form of modesty I can appreciate. Many far less successful young women than you can never stop talking about their triumphs. So you are unique in every way!"

About midway through the lunch he announced that she had provided him with an idea, and he would tell her all about it as soon as it was an established fact. If the idea worked out as he hoped it would they could discuss all the plans he had for her in comfort and leisure.

Janie seized upon the mention of plans for her, and tried discreetly to ascertain whether the contract for Vanessa was something that could be counted on. She was assured, with many not quite fatherly pats on the hand, that it was.

"My dear Vanessa," Winterton said, "how can you have the slightest doubt that you are not the very person I have been looking for for years?"

Janie felt relief well over her like the rising of a spring tide. Whatever happened now—even if she gave herself away!—she had his word. Although it would be better to have his signature on the all-important document, and that was an achievement that had yet to be worked for.

That night she watched Max Veldon conduct a beautifully balanced orchestra and forgot for the time being that she was not who she appeared to be, and could not even be herself. He was so superb, such a restrained showman as well as a musician, as he mounted the rostrum, and surely no man could look as he did in white tie and tails? A magnet which drew every pair of feminine eyes in the room!

The concert was being given in a setting that was

elegant without being restrained. The lushness, in fact, was almost overpowering, and practically every member of the audience reflected it. The women were lavishly besprinkled with diamonds and other precious stones, and the men all looked as if they devoted a generous share of their incomes to keeping their tailors in business.

The Russian princess, with a faint aura of remoteness and hauteur clinging to her, was perhaps the best dressed of all the women, and she wore little jewellery, yet was so unmistakably "someone" that Janie didn't have to ask to have her pointed out to her. Miss Calendar, who sat next to her, did however point her out in a rather loud whisper before the atmosphere was electrified by the appearance of the Austrian conductor, after which it was impossible for the attention to be diverted.

The evening was devoted to the music of Beethoven, in particular the *Emperor Concerto*, and Janie felt as if she was caught up in a world of purest magic and quite unalloyed bliss as she listened. Beethoven . . . the genius so revered by old Hermann Brandt, and whose story her own father had told in his book, *The Great Ones*. But Beethoven wasn't merely great, he was beyond all worldly criticism or approval. By simply sitting in her seat and listening to the rise and fall of the music, and watching those hands—every slightest

movement of which meant something to the orchestra—holding every other pair of eyes spellbound,
she felt that she was looking into the heart and
mind of the composer who had lived with tragedy,
and shared his moments of melancholy and his
ecstatic flights to the stars.

On her other side, in the row of plush-covered
chairs, with many conflicting but expensive per-
fumes floating in the atmosphere, yet scarcely a
rustle amongst the silks and satins and taffeta
underskirts that clothed the graceful nether limbs
of the female members of the audience, Rudi sat
and wore an utterly unreadable expression on his
face until the tension relaxed and the hand-clap-
ping became so violent that it shook the building.

Then he turned and glanced at Janie, whose
eyes were like stars. He said softly:

"So you enjoyed it? You really enjoyed it!"

"But of course." She gazed back at him in
astonishment. "I've never enjoyed anything so
much in my life! It was ... wonderful!"

"Even though it was Max who conducted? And
you can't have any reason to approve of Max,
when he holds you in such obvious contempt?"

"I——" Then she fell silent, feeling as if he had
plunged her into a sea of bewilderment. It didn't
matter whether she approved of Max Veldon or
not, he would still hold her in contempt, and he
would still be a wonderful musician. A distiller of

magic and a king among men . . . because of his powers.

She felt that she wanted to crawl to him and thank him for the wonder of her evening, and for the pleasure that almost everyone else had experienced, as she decided that there was nothing at all she could say to Rudi von Eisler in explanation of her attitude, and the thunderous applause went on and on. And when at last the impeccable figure in white tie and tails came down from his exalted pinnacle and mingled in the artists' room with the selected ones amongst the audience who either knew him well, or had been promised an introduction, she was there on the fringe of them and her eyes were bemused, but still glowing a little with admiration and wholehearted appreciation, when he abruptly noticed her.

To her astonishment she found that he was beside her, and looking at her rather keenly.

"You enjoyed it, yes?" he said, his accent more noticeable than usual because he himself was still treading a higher plane than the one ordinary mortals tread.

She tried to tell him how much she had enjoyed it.

He looked down at her more alertly still, as if something in her face had actually arrested his attention.

"The *Emperor* is one of your favourites, is that

it?" he said. "As," rather softly, "I remember it was of your father's. I told you I enjoyed his book, didn't I? And that I have it in my library?"

"I expect you have a wonderful library," she said, a little wistfully. "And no doubt a wonderful house, too?"

He smiled with a hint of amusement.

"As a matter of fact, I have two houses, and a flat—in Paris. Have you ever been to Paris?"

She shook her head.

"No."

"Then you must go there one day." He appeared to have forgotten that she was Vanessa Brandt, who had sung at the Opera House in Paris, and not Jane Dallas. "It has everything a capital should have, including atmosphere. If you have never walked down the Champs-Elysées on a day in spring you have never lived." He smiled at her, and it was an entirely new smile, softly brilliant like the smile he directed at the Princess Oranovski when he bent over her hand, and with something in it that had not been there for the Princess Oranovski. A hint of indulgence, of almost gentle humour. "And a young woman like you must start to live sooner or later, mustn't she?"

Janie lowered her eyes before his.

"For me this—impersonation—is starting to live," she said.

Instantly he frowned, and she realized she had

destroyed the moment of friendliness . . . perhaps for ever. He straightened his shoulders and stood up very stiffly.

"A good thing you reminded me!" he said. "I was in danger of mistaking you for a young woman with no other aspirations than to get the best out of life!" He bowed very formally as the Princess drew near. "Princess, may I present Miss Vanessa Brandt, whose singing has no doubt delighted you on various occasions. . . ."

CHAPTER VII

THEY went on to a party at the Princess's house, and Janie felt more and more bewildered. The music of the concerto was still running through her head, she had had a few moments' conversation with the man who was the lion of the evening, and those moments had surprised her. Then she was abruptly brought down to earth by her own reminder to him that she was something of a fraud, and as a result of the reminder he had been bluntly offensive.

She had travelled to the Princess's house in his chauffeur-driven car, but it was left to Rudi to entertain her. And for some reason Rudi was in an awkward mood.

"These affairs bore me," he remarked, when they were decanted at last. "Nothing but music, music, music, and adulation and adoration poured out over Max. It's like wading through a lot of sticky syrup."

"But music makes it possible for you to lead a fairly comfortable existence, doesn't it?" she replied, recollecting that he had once confessed to her that it was Max who provided him with all the frills of existence. "Without him what would you do?"

"Oh, get a job as a salesman, or something." He spoke moodily, and she smiled at the thought of him as a salesman, with his expensive tastes, and his disinclination—so far as she had been able to judge—for anything in the nature of real hard work. He was supposed to be employed by his brother, but she had not so far discovered that he did anything to justify the description "employee."

He was always beautifully dressed—usually with a flower in his buttonhole, like the maestro himself —and he was so devastatingly good-looking that members of the fair sex never failed to look twice when he passed by. If circumstances ever rendered it necessary he could become a beautiful gigolo, although his title would always prevent him from being referred to as a gigolo.

"I don't think I can see you as a salesman," she told him, when they were alone in a corner of one of the huge rooms, and she was sipping with caution a glass of champagne he had just put into her hand. "So I wouldn't quarrel with your brother if I were you."

He smiled rather wryly.

"Let's break out," he said suddenly. "Let's get away somewhere on our own, and enjoy ourselves for this one night at least!"

She regarded him thoughtfully.

"Do you know," she said, "that your brother has expressly forbidden me to have anything in the nature of an association with you?"

"So what?" he said softly, jeeringly. "He will cast you off and forget everything about you the moment we return to England, and that contract for Vanessa is safe, and yet you are careful to do exactly as he says? What have you to lose if Vanessa fails to get her contract? And, between you and me and the gatepost, her singing isn't what it used to be! If she gets the contract, she may not be able to fulfil it. Have you thought what happens then?" he asked still more softly.

She stared at him as if there was something about his lustrous dark eyes that fascinated her.

"You mean——?"

"That operation might not be a success, or— even if it is a success—it may take weeks before she has recovered sufficiently to sing again. If you sign a contract on Vanessa's behalf you'll be defrauding the public ... and you'll certainly be deceiving Abraham Winterton. He's the sort of man who has time for the best, and only the best ... never second-best!"

Janie continued to stare at him.

"I never thought of that. And I like Mr. Winterton."

"Judging by the attentions he has already paid

you he also likes you. I doubt very much whether
Vanessa would have scored quite such a personal
success."

"But she's beautiful——"

"So are you! Something that's much nicer than
beautiful ... lovely!"

"And she's ill," she said suddenly, anxiously.
"I've got to do the right thing for her."

"And the right thing for her might not be a contract that will tie her up to hours of work, even
although it may put money into her banking account! The right thing for Vanessa could be an
honest period of rest."

He took her by the elbow. Somewhere in the
house a trio composed of violin, harp and cello was
delighting the company, and the music came softly
to Janie's ears. She had a feeling that she would
always remember this night and the music.

"Let's disappear," Rudi urged her, his voice
soft and silken with coaxing. "I can tell that I've
thrown you into a kind of a quandary, and we can
talk the whole thing over somewhere where there
aren't so many people milling about. I know a
little down-town restaurant ... or we could take a
taxi and drive about for a while."

But she preferred the restaurant. She knew she
was asking for the sternest of rebukes when she
once more encountered Max Veldon, but all at
once it didn't seem to matter so much that Max

Veldon should rebuke her but that she herself should become really clear in her own mind about what she was doing. Why she was doing it, where it was leading her, and how it might recoil upon Vanessa.

And the only person she could discuss such an extraordinary situation with was the Baron von Eisler. Miss Calendar might have been willing to discuss it, but she would never do or say anything in opposition to the interests of her employer, Max Veldon. And as his one obsession was for Vanessa to get the Abraham Winterton contract, Miss Calendar was almost certainly a victim of the same sort of obsession.

The little down-town restaurant was small, but it had an excellent floor for dancing, and for the first time Janie found herself dancing with the man who had everything to commend him in the way of attractiveness, and who seemed to be extraordinarily attracted by her.

He held her very closely while they danced, and told her she was quite unlike anyone he had ever met before. He had met so many beautiful women, but they all bored him, and women who were dull and ordinary couldn't interest him for a moment. She was unique because she was such an extraordinary good actress, although she had never acted before in her life. She also, he believed, disliked enacting a role, and his brother had told him she was getting nothing for it. He couldn't believe that.

"He offered me a thousand pounds," Janie said dryly, while they danced.

"*He* offered you a thousand pounds, or Vanessa offered you a thousand pounds?"

"Mr. Veldon offered me a thousand pounds."

Rudi whistled.

"Then that proves something I've always suspected. Max has steered clear of women most of his life, apart from the odd entanglement, and he isn't the type of man who will ever marry. A wife and a family would be a nuisance to him . . . but he and Vanessa! I know he admires her enormously, and I always suspected he'd do anything he could to promote her career. *Now* I know that he'd even run the risk of getting himself in a spot of bother for her sake."

"What do you mean?" Janie asked, a somewhat distrait note in her voice. "A spot of bother?"

She was thinking . . . so he isn't the type who would marry! Well, it never even occurred to me that he is. A man who leads a life such as he leads, filled with adulation, oiled by applause, involving almost constant travel, would be most unsuited for married life.

Yet the thought brought a queer kind of disinclination to believe it in its train. It affected her in the same way that a sudden discord in the very middle of the *Emperor Concerto* would almost certainly have affected her.

The lights had gone down, and Rudi was holding her closer.

"You and I," he said softly, "we're the same type of person really, you know. Our beginnings were all right . . . I believe your father had quite a reputation as a music critic, hadn't he? But he doesn't appear to have left you any money. And my father made a thorough job of emptying the family coffers while he had the opportunity, which was most unfortunate for me, who came after him!"

He lowered his head, and she had the feeling that he might kiss her—for one instant the downward movement of that sleek dark head provided her with a sudden rising of excitement because he was such an attractive man, and it was the first time she had been brought into such close relationship with a man of his type—but he didn't do so. He merely allowed his lips to brush her hair lightly, and then led her back to their table on the edge of the floor.

"Don't worry about anything," he recommended. "And, whatever you do, don't worry about the outcome of this American week. I've got a plan for you, little one, and it might solve all your problems . . . possibly mine as well!"

She felt bewildered, and suddenly very weary, for she wasn't accustomed to keeping such late hours. More plans, she thought ... but she wasn't particularly interested in plans. They weren't really for her, and they could lead nowhere.

Not altogether to her surprise, Veldon was waiting for her when she got back to her hotel. He was pacing up and down the floor of the sitting-room, looking like an immaculately groomed tiger. Miss Calendar had obviously gone to bed and left her to face the music ... only this time it wasn't the *Emperor Concerto!*

"Where have you been?" he demanded.

She told him truthfully that his half-brother had taken her dancing.

His dark eyes surveyed her with almost sinister dislike.

"For a short while this evening I thought you were quite a pleasant young woman,' he told her. "But now I know that you're quite unreliable, and I was a fool to allow Vanessa to talk me into allowing you to attempt to get away with this dangerous experiment. Not only is it highly likely that you'll wreck her career, but you'll wreck mine."

"What do you mean?" she asked, feeling herself grow cold—although it was a suffocatingly hot night, and all the windows were wide because of it —under the balefulness of his look.

He moved nearer to her.

"Haven't you any sense?" he asked. "Don't you realize that we're treading the path of deception, and one false move can spell disaster? I know you're not Vanessa Brandt—I know that Vanessa Brandt is in London undergoing an operation—yet I'm introducing you to some of the most influential people I know *as* Vanessa Brandt. What do you suppose their opinion will be of me when they accidentally discover the truth? Accidentally or because of your stupid carelessness!"

She swallowed. She felt very tired, and the room was inclined to sway round her.

"I'm not careless," she defended herself. "In fact, I try very hard to be constantly on the alert. But it isn't easy."

"You don't make it any easier by courting deliberate risks. You slip away from a formal party to dance in some low dive with my half-brother, and as everyone knows Vanessa wouldn't be seen dead in that sort of place. She has her eyes always turned towards advancement . . . and that's sensible. And the last person she'd go dancing with is Rudi."

"Are you quite certain of that?" she asked, suddenly by no means certain herself.

"Absolutely certain," he answered.

She looked at him with heavy, bewildered eyes.

"I wish I knew," she said.

"What do you mean?" he asked. He moved

closer still to her and gripped her wrist. "What do you mean?" he repeated.

She made a helpless shrugging movement with her shoulders.

". . . Everything is a little beyond me. I don't understand why your half-brother, the Baron, wastes any time at all on me, and I don't understand why I ever agreed to do this—this despicable thing."

"Then you think it's despicable, deceiving people?"

"Of course."

Her eyes were so large and clear and truthful that he flung away from her. Then he came back.

"Listen to me," he said curtly. "Don't bother your head about the whys and the wherefores of all this. It's done now, and we're all in it together . . . myself, Rudi, Miss Calendar and you. And, of course, Vanessa. And you're the one who can give us all away . . . ruin everything for Vanessa. And if you ruin things for her I'll never forgive you!"

His fingers gripped her wrist so hard that she winced.

"I telephoned the nursing home in London to-night, and Vanessa was operated on this morning. Her convalescence is likely to take longer than we prepared ourselves for, and that means you've got to act the part you're acting now until she's fit. And you've got to work hard for her contract."

Janie said faintly:

"I don't think there's any doubt about the contract."

"Why?" He looked at her quickly. "What makes you think that?"

"At lunch today . . . Mr. Winterton said there isn't any doubt. He says he has plans—rather special plans—for Vanessa."

"H'm." He looked at her so closely, and so curiously, that she wondered what it was she had done now. In what particular way she had transgressed. But all at once his voice was quite calm and just a little puzzled as he said: "You're quite an efficient worker when you get down to it, aren't you? But all the same, I don't quite understand this prompt success. . . ."

He went on looking at her so curiously that she wrenched away her wrist and turned her back on him. She rubbed mechanically at the spot on her wrist where a bruise was already forming.

"If you don't mind," she said, rather falteringly, "I'd like to go to bed. . . ."

"Did I hurt you just now?" he asked, in the quietest and most controlled voice she had yet heard from him, and she turned round slowly and looked at him with one large bead of moisture clinging to her lashes.

"It doesn't matter."

He picked up her wrist and saw the bruise, and

all the redness surrounding it . . . undeniably the marks of his fingers.

"I'm sorry," he said unexpectedly. "I'm afraid I can be rather a brute when I . . . well, when I lose my temper—as I did just now."

"It doesn't matter," she repeated. She lifted her eyes and looked into the black, inscrutable eyes above her . . . only they weren't really inscrutable any longer, and they weren't angry. There was a definite gleam of apology in them, and something else that she didn't quite understand. She wondered—and then dismissed the thought—was it a hint of self-reproach?

"Mr. Veldon," she said breathlessly, "you can be sure of one thing. "I've started to play this part, and I'll carry on playing it . . . and I promise you I'll do nothing to endanger Vanessa—or you— again. However much it costs me, and if I mortgage my whole future happiness, I'll see that this thing works out—for you and Vanessa!"

CHAPTER VIII

THE next morning it was Abraham Winterton who was her early caller. He came into her sitting-room with a personal tribute of very dark red roses, and when Miss Calendar burst into the bathroom in an agitated manner to hurry Janie up, the exquisite scent of the roses followed her through the door.

"You'll have to get dressed quickly," Miss Calendar told her. "Mr. Winterton is here himself, and although he says I'm not to rush you he's simply bursting to see you. He says he must have a talk with you as soon as possible."

Janie scrambled out of the bath and dried herself on a rough bath-towel, and then darted through into her bedroom to complete a hurried toilet. Miss Calendar selected a dress for her—a simple flowered cotton, for once, in which she could hardly have looked more attractive—and chose her shoes, and clasped a neat row of pearls about her neck. Then she urged her agitatedly towards the sitting-room door.

"Don't keep him waiting," she begged. "This is really something, that he should come here at this hour to see you, and not just make an arrangement to meet you for lunch. Whatever you do, play up to him!"

Janie hardly heard her. She had a strange, sinking feeling at the base of her stomach, and she knew that this would prove a memorable morning for her. She didn't know quite why, but she did know it.

Winterton sprang up from his chair at sight of her. He could hardly have looked more debonair than he did in his light grey suit that was irreproachably tailored, and his jauntily flowing tie. For a man who didn't normally keep extremely early hours—save on important occasions—he looked remarkably fresh and alert, and almost boyishly good-looking.

"Vanessa!" He took her hand and kissed it; and then refused to release it. He drew her down on to a settee, and sat beside her, and her hand was retained between his well-cared-for, rather feminine hands. The brightness of his eyes as he took in every detail of her appearance confused her. "As usual, you are altogether charming," he told her. "In fact, this morning, although I have been inconsiderate enough to rush you, you are looking even more charming than usual. . . ." He touched the cotton dress. "Simplicity becomes you, my dear!"

Janie resisted the urge to tug her hand away from his—he smelled strongly of lavender toilet soap, and made her think of bath-tubs, and even nursery cleanliness—and tried to appear as if she was flattered by his compliments. But actually, at this beginning of another hot New York day, with so much dependent on her, she would not have felt flattered by anything.

"You look a trifle distrait," Winterton observed, just a shade reproachfully, and instantly she remembered how *much* depended on her, and called upon all her reserves to be as charming to him as possible.

"Please forgive me," she said, lying blatantly, "but my ankle hurt me last night, and I didn't sleep very well."

She certainly hadn't slept well, but it was not due to her ankle. Winterton instantly looked concerned.

"Forgive *me*," he begged her. "I'm afraid I forgot that it might be troubling you still." He looked down at the slender ankle, encased in a sheer stocking, and his brow clouded. "I don't like to think of you being troubled by anything—certainly not enduring pain. I wish you had allowed me to get my doctor to look at it."

"No, no," she said quickly—almost too hastily. "It really is very much better, but I'm afraid I danced rather a lot last night. ..."

Immediately she wished she hadn't said that.

"You danced?" But to her relief he didn't ask her where, or with whom, she danced. Instead he smiled at her, a warm and uncannily understanding smile. "I like to think of you dancing," he told her. "I like to think of you enjoying yourself. Someone like you should dance, and have a good time, and be utterly carefree. I'm not at all sure I would saddle you with the formidable daily routine of a singer, or the responsibility for entertaining the public."

"But my career is important," she pointed out.

"Is it?" He continued to smile at her. "Is it so important, Vanessa?"

She felt vaguely afraid as she met his eyes ... vaguely alarmed.

"Naturally, it is the most important thing in life to me," she told him.

He looked down thoughtfully at her slim fingers, that were tightly clasped in her lap. His eyes roved round the room, with V for Vanessa in an arrangement of flowers—his own flowers—in a corner, and on a gold-cigarette-case that lay on a table. Her slim sharkskin handbag, that also had a huge golden V.B. on it, lay beside them on the settee.

"In that case," he asked quietly, "why did you not seek to make a career of your own, my dear? What tempted you to step into another woman's shoes, instead of looking for a pair of suitable shoes for yourself?"

She gasped. He knew! And she could say nothing at all to answer him.

"Don't panic, my dear," he said even more

gently. "I'm amazed that Veldon thought I could be so easily taken in, although I'm sure he had his reasons for running a risk of this sort. I have never met Miss Vanessa Brandt, but her appearance can't really be very similar to yours. You no doubt have her features, and her colouring, but she is a woman of experience. . . . And you, my dear, are you!"

She felt him take her hand, and she permitted him to retain it, a limp and petrified thing in his warm clasp. The scent of his lavender toilet soap —or was it his shaving-cream?—no longer affronted her in any way, and she was amazed because he was not harsh, or annoyed, or even critical. She was still more amazed that he went on talking to her in such a soothing voice.

"Why did you do it?" he asked. "And where is the real Vanessa?"

"In London," she answered, licking her lips. "In a clinic, where she underwent an operation yesterday morning. I took her place because she wanted your contract, and she was afraid that if you knew about the trouble she was having with her throat you wouldn't consider she was fit for a contract."

He sat very silent for a few minutes, and then he asked:

"And Veldon? He is in the secret, of course? No doubt the whole thing was his idea?"

"No, it wasn't." She denied it almost vehemently. "It was Vanessa's idea, because she wanted the contract . . . no one else's, and therefore no one else can be held responsible. Except me," she added, with a catch in her voice. "I ought to have realized that no one could possibly mistake me for Vanessa."

"Oh, but they have," he assured her. "I don't think anyone save myself has had any doubts whatsoever."

She realized that she ought to be relieved, but she wasn't. He stood up and started to walk briskly up and down the confined limits of the hotel sitting-room.

"You can defend Veldon," he said, with a frown between his brows, "but it doesn't surprise me that he lent himself to this. Vanessa—Miss Brandt—was discovered by him and made famous by him, and in addition he may have other, more personal, reasons for wishing to further her career." He looked at Janie as if trying to find out whether she knew, but she shook her head.

"I know nothing about the relationship between Miss Brandt and Mr. Veldon," she assured him.

He said nothing. He continued his pacing up and down.

"And I'm sure Mr. Veldon didn't want to have anything to do with deceiving you," she put in with a note of almost pleading anxiety in her voice.

"Please, Mr. Winterton," she begged, "you must believe that."

He smiled suddenly and came across to her.

"I'll believe anything you care to tell me," he reassured her, "except that you're Vanessa Brandt. And, by the way," he wanted to know, once more taking his place beside her on the settee, "what really is your name? What may I call you when no one else is likely to overhear?"

She gazed at him hopefully.

"You mean that you won't give me away? That you'll go on pretending?"

"We'll see," he replied, smiling as he might have smiled at a child he was humouring. "But before I arrive at any decision of that sort you must tell me your name . . . the name which is really and truly yours."

"Jane Dallas," she answered.

"Ah," he said, softly. "I like that. Jane Dallas! Somehow it suits you much more than Vanessa." Then he took both her hands determinedly, and gripped them strongly. "Jane, I could make matters unpleasant for you, but believe me that is not my intention. I suppose I could make things pretty awkward for Veldon, but I won't do that, either . . . if I get what I want. And I want you, Jane. I want to marry you!"

"What?" she gasped.

He repeated very solemnly, "I want to marry

you. You're the first young woman I've ever met who has filled me with an almost instantaneous desire to take a wife, and you're the first young woman who has it in her power to make me bitterly unhappy if you refuse. But you won't refuse, will you, Jane?" very softly indeed. "For if you'd the courage to come out here as Vanessa Brandt you've the courage to marry me—a man you hardly know! And if you disappoint me cruelly by turning me down I'll have to think twice about that contract for Vanessa . . . the real Vanessa. And then there's this piece of gross deception permitted by Max Veldon . . . a man very much in the public eye. It won't do him very much good if the truth leaks out, will it? You know the old saying . . . *The higher you climb, the farther you can fall!*"

"You're threatening me," she said dully. "You're threatening Mr. Veldon, through me."

His smile was almost whimsical.

"You can put it like that if you wish. But a man who is fighting for his own interests has to use ugly weapons sometimes!"

CHAPTER IX

Miss Calendar fussed somewhat unnecessarily about the sitting-room while Janie waited for the door to open and Max Veldon to stand looking in upon them, one eyebrow rather questioningly raised.

Janie looked so taut that Miss Calendar, no fool, realized that something in the nature of a crisis had arisen. But Janie refused to discuss it, and the one thing she had said urgently when Abraham Winterton departed was that they must get in touch with Mr. Veldon.

"But I haven't any real idea where he is," his secretary protested. "He could be in any one of half·a dozen places, and if it's really urgent I'll telephone and see if I can run him to earth. But I'd like to be convinced that it *is* urgent."

"It is," Janie assured her quietly. "It's extremely urgent."

Miss Calendar sent her a long look, remembered how exceptionally affable Mr. Winterton had been when·he took his departure, and wished she had some clue to what had happened.

Max Veldon was not in any of the half-dozen places, and a few other telephone calls refused to establish contact with him. But after lunch he telephoned the suite himself, and Miss Calendar said at once that Janie was very anxious to see him.

"*Very* anxious," she repeated.

At the other end of the line the conductor asked curtly:

"Anything wrong?"

"Not so far as I know," Miss Calendar replied. "But you'd better get here as quickly as possible all the same."

Max Veldon arrived about twenty minutes later. He was wearing a very debonair light grey suit, and there was a half-opened pale pink rosebud in his buttonhole. He looked as if he had been torn from a lunch at which he had been prepared to enjoy himself; but he was no longer prepared to enjoy himself in the slightest when he looked across the room at Janie.

"Well?" he said.

Janie looked at Miss Calendar, who took the hint and evaporated as quickly and silently as she could. Max Veldon strode into the middle of the room and extracted a carnation from a vase on a table. He wielded it as if it was a baton as he addressed himself to Janie.

"You'd better tell me the truth, the whole truth, and nothing but the truth," he advised her grimly.

She did, and she had the satisfaction for the first time of seeing him look completely and absolutely astounded. He sat down on the arm of a chair after giving a careful hitch to his trousers—she realized that it was purely force of habit that caused him to do so—and stared at her as if he was seeing her also for the first time, and was attempting to assimilate all that was there to be taken in.

"You really expect me to believe, Fräulein," he said at last—and it was noticeable that under stress his English became much more mixed up with his native German—"that a man who is so wealthy, and so personally attractive to women that he can have his pick of them, has asked you—*you* to be his wife?"

Janie's pale skin became stained with the flush of humiliation. Even in such a moment he had the power to make her feel insignificant, and even worthless.

"I have just told you that Mr. Winterton proposed to me quite seriously this morning," she said through stiff, resentful lips. "He asked me to be his wife. In fact, I have no alternative to becoming his wife if your reputation and Vanessa's are not to—well, suffer badly! And Vanessa will lose her contract."

Max Veldon's brows puckered in perplexity. He had noticed the rush of colour to the girl's cheeks, and to her surprise it was an apology he offered her before he said anything else.

."You mustn't mistake my intention when I say .something at which you can take offence, Janie...."
And it was the very first time he had called her Janie. "I am quite certain there are lots of men who would be delighted to marry you, but Winterton is not just any man. Not merely can he pick and choose, but he can pick and choose all the time. If he wants a wife who is supremely beautiful he can pick a wife who is supremely beautiful, and if he wants talent and beauty ... why, then, talent and beauty are both his. But you are a young woman with no particular talents and your background is obscure. He isn't even interested in your background ... he just wishes to marry you! Why?"

"Because he is annoyed with Vanessa, perhaps. Annoyed with you." She looked away from him as she spoke, and the muscles of her slender white throat contracted.

"My dear child, don't talk as if you've never even begun to grow up." Then he laughed, rather strangely, and stood up and started to pace about the room. She watched his pantherish strides as if they fascinated her. "What a triumph for you!" He glanced over his shoulder at her, almost appreciatively. "The little girl from the antique shop to the first Mrs. Winterton ... the *first* Mrs. Winterton, mind!"

"Don't be absurd," Janie returned, with the same taut look.

"But I am not being absurd," he told her. "It has happened before, of course . . . someone like you bowling over an experienced man. Someone young, and fresh, and charming. Yes," he conceded, turning to stare at her openly. "You are undoubtedly very charming." He inclined his dark head several times to give emphasis to his words.

Janie felt as if her whole being quivered with resentment as she met his eyes. She couldn't believe that he wasn't mocking her.

"But Winterton must be somewhere in his forties, and you are a young woman in her early twenties. It is too much like May and December to appeal to me, so I'm afraid I can't offer you my congratulations."

Janie felt as if she would choke.

"I'm not asking you to congratulate me! I'm merely trying to make you understand that the position is serious! For some reason Mr. Winterton *means* that if I don't marry him Miss Brandt will not receive a contract."

"The reason is obvious. He's in love with you," he said suavely.

"But what about . . . your reputation?" she inquired, marvelling at his lack of concern, his strange but interested detachment.

He shrugged.

"Oh, I suppose he could do me a certain amount of harm . . . but the thought of it doesn't really upset me. And Vanessa will survive without her contract."

"But only yesterday you told me——"

He shrugged once more, and waved one of his slim hands carelessly.

"Naturally she'll be disappointed, but she wouldn't expect you to marry in order to prevent her disappointment." His expression grew sharper, more alert. "And you're not seriously contemplating marrying Winterton in order to safeguard my reputation and further Vanessa's interests, are you?" he asked, going closer to her and peering into her face.

"I am," she answered, feeling the instinct to back away from him, but not doing so. "Only yesterday you said that if I failed you—if I endangered Vanessa's future and made you a subject for gossip— you would never forgive me, and so I told Mr. Winterton that I was immensely flattered by his proposal, and would marry him whenever he wishes."

For the second time she felt his fingers encompassing her wrist, bruising it cruelly.

"You little fool!" he exclaimed. "I can't believe you!"

"Nevertheless it's true." Her grey eyes were quiet and unrevealing as she gazed at him. "I said I would marry him because there didn't seem to be any alternative, and he's giving a party tonight at

which our engagement will be announced. The
wedding will take place practically immediately,
because he has plans for a somewhat unusual
honeymoon . . . but that concerns you!"

Veldon didn't seem to be listening. He gripped
her by her other hand and almost dragged her up
against him.

"Tell me something," he ordered. "Are you
tempted by Winterton's money? . . . his position?"

"Of course not," she gasped back, her expression
of astonishment so obviously genuine that it should
have convinced him. "How can you imagine such
a thing?"

"I can, easily," he replied tersely. "When a
young woman like you decides to marry a man
twice her age on some trumped-up pretext. . . ."

"It isn't a pretext," she declared furiously—and
for the first time she was so angry with him that all
the colour left her face, and she started to shake.
"I think you are absolutely detestable—and I think
Miss Vanessa Brandt is detestable, too, otherwise
she wouldn't despise her own humble beginnings
and involve you in something that could be fatal to
your career! But so far as I'm concerned your
career is important only because, if anything happens to it, I am the one you will blame! You have
already said things I'm not likely to forget."

"What do you mean by Vanessa's humble beginnings?" he demanded, ignoring the rest.

"Her father isn't an antique dealer; he keeps a second-hand shop in a part of London you would be most unlikely to frequent. But I was his assistant, and I'm very devoted to him."

"Then why didn't you stay with him instead of being tempted by a trip to New York?"

"I wasn't tempted." Active dislike invaded her expression as she stared up at him. "I was talked into it, and also, I suppose, I was sorry for poor old Hermann. There was a time when his daughter was everything to him, and he made sacrifices for her—he went on living where he still does live, in a tiny flat over his sordid shop, in order that she should be sent away to school and given a good education. And later there was all the expense of training her voice . . . and now she despises him!" Her voice quivered with indignation. "She wasn't even prepared to spend one night in the flat with him before she went into the nursing home!"

Max Veldon accepted this piece of information without comment. And he went on gripping her wrists.

"And you want me to believe that there was nothing—*nothing* about this trip to New York that tempted you?" he insisted.

She was about to reply contemptuously that a few smart clothes and the opportunity to mix with some superficially smart people would never tempt her, when her native truthfulness got the better of her, and she added a piece of information that did surprise him.

"If I was tempted at all, it was because you were a kind of hero of mine . . . someone I worshipped from afar. Like hundreds and thousands of other women who sit in your audiences and watch you I. thought you were wonderful. And it seemed almost too good to be true that I could spend a few days in your company, and have them to treasure for the rest of my life. But my very first interview with you was rather like a shock."

"Yes," he· said quietly, watching her closely. "Why was it a shock?"

"Because it revealed the feet of clay! As a conductor you were—you are—wonderful; but as a man in the life of a young woman like myself there is nothing wonderful about you. You took an almost instantaneous dislike to me, and you never even pretended that it was otherwise. Why should you? When you are you, and I am—well, just me! Why should a great man like yourself put himself out to be polite and considerate to a girl whose rightful background is the shop where she is employed?"

He stood regarding her almost broodingly.

"The answer to that," he replied at last, "is that we can all of us rise above our backgrounds. I don't see you fitting in very well in a junk shop . . . not permanently, anyway!"

He started to pace up and down the room, as she had seen him do often before. Then he came back to her and spoke with a strange earnestness.

"There isn't the smallest reason why you should marry Winterton. . . ."

"Except that Vanessa is ill at the moment, and counting upon her contract." She looked him straight in the eyes. "I'm not really concerned with your reputation, Mr. Veldon—I'm sure your fans will be faithful to you whatever Mr. Winterton might say about you. But Vanessa has nothing but a long period of convalescence to look forward to at the moment, and if in addition to losing her contract she gets talked about. . . . Well, women are vulnerable, in a way that men are not vulnerable, and she might find it difficult to get back on her feet again."

"So you'll sacrifice yourself for Vanessa?" dryly, "but not for me!"

She sighed.

"You won't believe it's a sacrifice. And it isn't, really, of course. . . . It's the most extraordinary piece of good fortune." She looked down at the belt of her dress that she had been maltreating ruthlessly with her fingers. "I suppose it's because I haven't had time yet to get used to the idea that I'm not quite overwhelmed."

"But when the truth has had an opportunity to sink in, you really will be—overwhelmed? You might even convince yourself that it will be a simple matter to fall in love with Winterton?"

"I don't know anything about love," she answered without looking at him.

He made an abrupt movement and turned away.

"Lucky for you. Love is a complication best avoided. And if you don't really need it, well then, I suppose you can always do without it!" At the door he paused to look back at her. "But I'm sorry I made such an unfavourable impression on you when we met for the first time—away from the glamour of the concert hall, that is!"

Across the width of the room her grey eyes attempted an apology.

"And I'm sorry I had to admit to you that you were once a kind of hero of mine. For two years, to be quite truthful!"

"But a hero with feet of clay! Too bad!" He shook his head mockingly.

That night he was one of the first to offer his congratulations to the happy couple when Abraham Winterton made his announcement to a crowded room.

It was the vast room at his flat—the room with the swaying gold curtains that made a noise like the whispering of the night breeze itself when it stirred them with hot and breathless fingers.

"I am the happiest man in the world tonight,"

Winterton declared. "For the loveliest woman in the world has consented to marry me. Me, a hardened bachelor!"

If the majority of his friends were surprised, all they betrayed was delight. They fawned upon Janie, although her eyes met his almost appealingly once or twice—but the Baron von Eisler whispered to Janie in astonishment when he got her alone.

"But what happens to Vanessa when the truth leaks out? I mean, it will be Jane Dallas who becomes Mrs. Winterton, and unless you're contemplating committing a serious fraud"—she gathered he was not in the least delighted by the turn events had taken—"you'll have to be honest with the registrar, at least. And I can't see Vanessa allowing another woman to get married in her name!"

"I have no intention of marrying in any name but my own," she replied stiltedly. "Mr. Winterton— Abraham," she corrected herself selfconsciously, "has a plan to simplify the present position."

"Then it will have to be a very good plan," the Baron observed laconically. "So many people appear to have been taken in by your impersonation of Vanessa."

And he glanced about him as if half relishing the thought of their changed expressions should someone suddenly drop a bomb in their midst, and reveal the truth about the future Mrs. Winterton.

Over by one of the enormous windows Winterton outlined his plan to Veldon, after bluntly admitting to him that he had known the truth for some time.

"I don't blame you, Veldon," he said. "Women have a way of getting what they want when they want it badly enough, and I gather that Vanessa wants to sign on the dotted line with me very badly indeed!"

The Austrian conductor was standing very stiffly, looking very dark and distinguished and foreign in his evening things. Janie, who had managed to fight her way through the crush to be nearer to them, thought that he also looked as if every muscle in his body was taut, and he himself battling with a strong sensation of distaste and disapproval.

Although why he should be disapproving now she couldn't think, when the situation was about to be resolved for him.

Winterton, not noticing she was near, dug him rather playfully in the ribs.

"Of course, I also realize that there's a strong personal element in this. A favourite pupil become an outstanding star, in addition to being an exceptionally beautiful woman! You naturally want the best of all possible worlds for her, and one day very likely for yourself?" Another dig in the ribs. "There comes a time in the lives of most of us men when we feel the need to take a wife ... and start a family. You and your Vanessa, and me and my Jane"—he suddenly looked round for her anxiously —"will have to get together over this!"

He extended a hand eagerly when he caught sight of Janie, but she was breathlessly watching the conductor's face to see if, just for one moment, he might betray himself. Even a momentary flicker of relief would confirm what she believed, but there was not even the suspicion of a flicker of relief. Nothing but an unnatural coldness and calm—and distaste.

"Ah, so there you are, Jane!" Winterton exclaimed. "I've been trying to make Veldon realize that there's nothing really to worry about. You and I are going to get married—soon!—and that contract will go to the real Vanessa as soon as she's fit to sign it. But there's something I want in exchange for keeping up the necessary deception a bit longer."

He looked at the conductor with the expression of a keen businessman driving a fairly reasonable bargain.

"I want you to give Jane away at the wedding, Veldon, and I want you to let us have that castle of yours—*Schloss*, I believe you call it—in the Austrian Alps for our honeymoon. I once stayed with you there for a week-end, and it caught my fancy. I thought, if ever I get married, I'll ask Veldon to let me bring my bride here. And now I'm getting married, and I'll have to be close to Vienna for a time, so it will suit me admirably. Is that okay?"

Veldon looked long and strangely at Janie.

"I'll let you have the *Schloss,* but you can count me out at the wedding. Weddings and I do not agree with one another. . . . Perhaps because I'm a confirmed bachelor!"

And he turned on his heel and left them.

"Confirmed bachelor my foot!" Winterton exclaimed, as he looked after him with a faint puckering of his brows. "Everyone knows that he and the Brandt. . . ." Then he shrugged his shoulders. "Ah, well, perhaps it's she who isn't keen on marriage. These career women are all alike, and they'll sell their soul sometimes to further their interests. No wonder he looks a bit grim."

Then he looked down, beaming devotedly at Janie.

"How glad I am that you're just you, Janie, and you've no interest in a career. I couldn't have fallen for you as I have done if you'd been a career-woman, for I want my wife to think of nothing but me!"

CHAPTER X

JANIE felt as if she had fallen into a trap, and it was now securely fastened so that she couldn't escape from it.

When she saw that look in Winterton's eyes, and heard the slightly husky note in his voice as he told her that in future she was to think only of him, the doors of the trap swung shut. When he put his hand on her arm and urged her to escape from the crowded room with him because, although they were engaged, she hadn't so far allowed him to kiss her, or take advantage of any of the privileges of a fiancé, the key turned in the lock.

"Oh, no!" she protested, feeling as if panic rose in her in an actual tide. "I'm so terribly tired to-night!"

It was true, and every moment of the last few days had been so exhausing that all at once she felt as if she was being drained of her strength, and unless someone came to her rescue and made it possible for her to return to normality and obscurity she couldn't possibly go on putting up a pretence of any sort or kind.

"And it's so hot!"

It was, breathlessly, suffocating hot, and Winterton took pity on the sudden whiteness of her face, and the blankness of her expression, and agreed to take her straight back to her hotel and allow her to rest and recover from the suddenness of everything.

"I suppose it has been a bit of a strain for you, acting the part of Vanessa," he said. "But you won't have to act the part much longer, for when we get to Vienna, there won't be any point in it. Vienna is Vanessa's home ground, and we'll just let it be given out that she was taken ill in London and is recovering in a nursing home. You will be booked in at Sacher's Hotel as Jane Dallas."

"But you've announced tonight that you're engaged to Vanessa Brandt!"

He shrugged.

"And have you never heard of a beautiful opera singer changing her mind? By the time we get to Vienna I shall have been cruelly dropped by Vanessa, and you will have consoled me. My adorable little Jane!" He allowed one of his rather womanish hands to rest for a moment on her bare shoulder, and she couldn't prevent herself shrinking from his touch. "Jane, who is to become my wife!" with an inflexible note in his voice.

"You are not afraid that I . . . shall drop you?" she inquired in a faint voice.

He laughed, rather an unpleasant laugh.

"I don't think you will do that, my dear. You are too nice . . . too genuine. You entered into a kind of bargain with Miss Brandt, and you will keep your side of the bargain. Knowing that she is ill you won't do anything to hurt her still further."

"But supposing her health isn't good enough for her to take up the contract?"

"Then we'll see that she has a most enjoyable convalescence, and put as many plums in her path in future as we can. I've already telegraphed to the nursing home that all is well, and she has nothing to worry about save a quick recovery to complete health and excellent voice, and by this time there will be as many flowers in her room as you had when you arrived here."

Janie felt the bars of the cage begin to press on her.

"You have a very complete belief in me, haven't you?" she inquired dryly.

"Very complete," he assured her. "Otherwise I wouldn't have asked you to marry me! I'm not an impressionable boy, you know, my dear," he added quietly.

Janie bit her lip.

"But why do we have to keep in such close touch with—with Mr. Veldon? If you really do wish to marry me, why can't we got right away somewhere where he——?"

Winterton glanced at her quickly.

"You dislike him?" he asked. "You find him stiff-necked and impossible?"

"I don't think he has ever approved of me."

"Nonsense, my dear," he replied, with a gleam of humour in his eyes. "I don't believe there is a man in the world who could really and truly disapprove of you. But I know what you mean about Veldon. . . . There's an arrogance about him that's a bit difficult to swallow at times. As a musician, however, he's in a class by himself, and I've got to work with him in the next few weeks. And he's about the only man in the world who can handle Vanessa Brandt, so if I'm going to use her I've got to use Veldon."

"But do we have to stay at his *Schloss?*"

At that he caught her hand.

"Wait till you've seen it," he said. "It's a fairy-tale place, perched on the side of a mountain and overlooking a valley—a valley full of blue lakes and rivers. You'll smell the scent of pine woods from dawn till dusk, see snow lying on the high peaks that lies there from one year's end to the other. If two people want to spend a honeymoon somewhere . . . well, that's the spot!"

Janie wanted to cry out bewilderedly that a few days ago she hadn't dreamed of marrying anyone, and certainly not of having a honeymoon with a stranger. Much worse than a stranger! . . . A man in whom she wasn't even remotely interested, and knew that she could never be interested.

Whereas the owner of the *Schloss.* . . .

She forced herself to stop thinking along such lines. She was even slightly amazed at herself that she should think such thoughts. Max Veldon disliked her, and she disliked him. He was brutal and cruel, and the only woman he was really interested in was Vanessa Brandt.

He was in love with Vanessa, otherwise he wouldn't have risked his reputation to please her.

And unless she, Jane, pleased Abraham Winterton, his reputation was still not safe!

Not entirely safe, but not in as much danger as Vanessa's future, for a reputation such as he had built up could not be destroyed by a little malicious gossip. But to a man with his arrogant attitude to life, his cool pride, the disclosure of a certain amount of weakness would not be pleasant.

He would find it hard to live down, and wherever he went the admission of weakness would go with him. People would talk behind their hands, and their smiles would hold a hint of criticism. The idol would have developed feet of clay, and although it didn't matter if a girl like Jane Dallas made the discovery that he had feet of clay, it would matter very much indeed if the world became aware of them. The world of music, wherein he had hitherto held so secure a place, and which was his world . . . his bright, secure, and all-important world!

Jane knew that having committed herself to something irresponsible—or rather, allowed herself to be over-persuaded into doing something irresponsible—she couldn't let Vanessa down, and she couldn't permit a hint of tarnish to mar that scintillating reputation which Veldon had built up for himself. Especially when, while there was still an opportunity to withdraw, she had accepted a challenge that she wouldn't fail Vanessa, and that the support Veldon lent to her would not recoil on his own head.

She had a shrewd suspicion that, for some purely personal reason, Winterton would enjoy exposing Veldon as something in the nature of a fraud . . . just as she had a very strong suspicion that Rudi von Eisler wouldn't hesitate to conspire against his half-brother if it were to his own advantage. Therefore, while not entirely believing in the finality of the thing she had done, and the linking of her name with Winterton's, she arrived with him in Vienna and was instantly caught up in a far more fantastic whirl than that which had shaken her in New York.

New York was prosaic, but Vienna was like the coming to life of a fairy-tale—a real fairy-tale.

Sacher's Hotel, where a suite was booked for her, was a modern hotel with its feet firmly established in the past. It had all the amenities of the present day and age, but the splendours of the past were inescapable. Gilt and plush, oak and damask . . . Janie had the feeling that she had been offered a part in a lush musical of the Léhar period when she saw her own private sitting-room for the first time, and dined with her fiancé in the hotel dining-room that night.

They dined, for once, alone, for Veldon, who had accompanied them from New York, had gone straight to his own flat from the airport, and Miss Calendar had had the tact to say that she would enjoy a tray in her own room. Rudi, back in his own element, had temporarily disappeared . . . Janie hoped very much that it would be a lengthy disappearance, for the shatteringly handsome Baron, with his mocking, knowing eyes, frightened her sometimes.

And she was fairly certain he had many friends in Vienna who would welcome him back . . . particularly feminine friends.

Winterton expressed himself as delighted that he and Janie were able to dine alone.

"I would have liked to stop off in Paris for a while, and you could have bought yourself a trousseau there; but Vienna is a wonderful place for women—perhaps even more than Paris it caters for women—and you can go shopping tomorrow as early as you feel like it."

He fondled her hand, where it rested on the

satin damask of the tablecloth, and she instantly withdrew it as if she had been stung.

At the hurt look in his eyes she apologized.

"I'm sorry . . . I didn't quite realize what I was doing!"

His eyes narrowed a little.

"That's all right, sweetheart. I rather gather you're a little shy—another thing about you I adore!—and you're not used to being engaged yet. For that matter, neither am I," smiling very attractively. "I haven't even bought you a ring yet," reaching out and touching her hand again. "But we'll go shopping tomorrow together and remedy that omission."

"Oh, no!" she exclaimed, experiencing an odd sensation like horror at the thought of wearing the badge of their relationship on her finger. His ring! . . . There was something horribly final and irrevocable about wearing a man's ring. "Oh, no," she repeated, rather more faintly.

He smiled.

"Diamonds or rubies," he inquired, "emeralds or pearls? What are your favourite stones?"

"I—I haven't any!"

His smile grew broader.

"Soon you'll be quite a connoisseur. I shall load you with so many trinkets that you won't know what to do with them, and that goes for clothes, too. You must choose masses of them."

"You mean that you'll—pay for them?"

"Of course," almost complacently. "I shall pay for everything you do, wear, eat, or desire from now on."

She felt ridiculously appalled—considering that less than a week ago she hadn't had a sufficient amount of money to buy herself a modest outfit of clothes.

"I—I'm not married to you yet," she heard herself say in a thin thread of a voice that was rendered less audible by the sudden explosion of a champagne cork. "It isn't customary for a man to buy even a fiancée everything she needs until—until he is married to her!"

She realized that his laughter was both amused and humouring.

"What a girl!" he exclaimed. "What a delightful girl!" Then, almost tenderly: "We shall be married so soon that you won't have time to get used to being a fiancée, so we don't need to trouble ourselves with the way in which a fiancée should behave." He lifted his glass to her. "To us, my darling! To our whole future!"

At the far end of the restaurant the *maître d'hôtel* bowed a couple to a table, and the faint stir caused Janie to look round slowly. Immediately she wished that she hadn't, for the man in faultless evening dress, with very sleek dark hair and an air of being utterly removed from the rest of common humanity, was Max Veldon, and the woman he saw carefully seated was a Viennese beauty with a Viennese flair for the right sort of dress to become a redhead, and a melting smile for the man who was to dine with her.

Janie heard Winterton say something softly:

"That man certainly knows how to pick them! I don't think I've ever seen him with a fairly ordinary woman, and never in any circumstances a dowdy one!"

Janie felt her whole body grow a trifle hot as she recalled the way in which Veldon's remote dark eyes had once flickered over her disparagingly, and his remark concerning the simple outfit she was wearing:

"You certainly will have to wear very different clothes!"

Tonight she was wearing something rather simple, but such a delicate shade of faint rose pink that she looked like the heart of a china rose herself. Her golden hair was twisted into one of Vanessa Brandt's favourite lightly coiled knots low on the nape of her neck, and in her ears there were pearl studs. Otherwise she was without adornment, whereas the Viennese woman who was with Veldon was a blaze of iridescent stones like diamonds.

Before allowing himself to be seated Veldon glanced over at the table at which Winterton and his fiancée were seated. He bowed—a formal, rather

austere little bow which did no more than acknow-
ledge them—before giving all his attention to the
lovely lady who expected it.

Janie looked round quickly at the table in front
of her, heard another champagne cork give a light
and exciting "pop," and Winterton murmur:

"Veldon is back on his home ground. I wonder
whether he misses Vanessa very much, or whether
the charmer he is with will take her place very
satisfactorily tonight?"

Janie said nothing. She picked up her own champagne glass with slightly shaking fingers and gulped
at it, while somewhere deep in the heart of the
hotel some gypsy violins began to play softly and
seductively.

CHAPTER XI

It was in a shop sparkling with every sort of gem and full of deferential assistants that she saw Veldon again, and that was about the middle of the following morning.

The size of her finger had been carefully noted, and trays of rings were on the glass-topped counter beside which she and her fiancé were standing. Winterton was holding her hand with a reverence which could have indicated that it was made of porcelain, and he was murmuring something about pearls and a hope that she wasn't superstitious because one very large pearl surrounded by diamonds would look perfect on the slender third finger of her left hand, when she glanced up and met the eyes of the conductor.

It was rather like the night before, only this morning there was a cool look of amusement in the aloof dark eyes. He came over and bowed formally —as also on the night before—and if anything he was rather more impeccable than usual, with a flower in his buttonhole, and a certain casual air of jauntiness that in some way wounded Janie.

"Ah," he exclaimed, with dry amusement in his voice, "the ring! The all-important ring! I hope

you are savouring to the full the intense significance
of this moment, Miss Brandt?"

His eyes flickered over her, and she realized that
the one thing he was doing was enjoying the awk-
wardness of the situation for her, the acute embar-
rassment of it. With intense uneasiness at heart,
and by this time frightened awareness of the net
that was closing round her, she wondered why he
took such badly concealed pleasure in watching the
uneasiness in her eyes, the lack of interest she dis-
played while surrounded by so many costly and
scintillating trifles that should delight the heart of
a normal woman.

Maybe he thought she was a very normal
woman, and was putting on this pose for her
benefit.

As she thought that she saw Winterton frown.

"There is no need any longer to refer to Janie as
Miss Brandt," he said. "Since her arrival in Vienna
she has regained her own personality, and no one
should know better than you that here she would
never be mistaken for Vanessa."

He sounded irritated, as if some of Veldon's
malicious satisfaction had reached him, too, and he
resented it. Veldon merely smiled imperturbably.

"That is so very true," he agreed. "Here in
Vienna no one can impersonate Vanessa."

"But you allowed her to be impersonated in New
York," Winterton snapped. "And I must say—

although it has all turned out very much to my advantage—I do think you might have picked on someone a little less vulnerable than Janie to carry out the impersonation."

Veldon's eyes grew very cool.

"I had nothing whatever to do with it," he assured the impresario. "The whole piece of deception was an arrangement agreed upon by Vanessa and Miss Dallas, and at no time did it have my blessing."

"But you were perfectly well aware that it was in Miss Brandt's interests and not Janie's when you consented to try and put the thing over on the public," Winterton snapped again. "To say nothing of a deliberate intention to take me in, also! However," seeming to regret losing his temper, "as I have already remarked, I have no real cause for complaint, for I'm the lucky one, and but for Vanessa's throat trouble I would have still been looking for a wife. Now, at last, I've found one," squeezing Janie's hand, "and I don't want to appear critical of anything that led up to my finding her!"

"That, at least, is forbearing of you," Veldon remarked, with somewhat tight lips, and Winterton administered one of his jovial pokes in the ribs.

"What are you here for, anyway?" he demanded. "Don't tell me you want to buy something pretty for that ravishing creature you were with last night? I don't mind confessing that if I hadn't already met Janie I'd have got you to introduce me!"

Veldon turned away, as if the atmosphere of the jeweller's was either too warm, and he needed some fresh air, or he was suddenly and acutely bored.

"The lady I was with is an old friend," he replied stiffly.

Winterton's eyes twinkled.

"I've heard that one before," he remarked. "But it's sometimes a good thing to run into an old friend!"

They went on with the selection of Janie's ring, and Veldon inquired about some cuff-links that were being repaired for him. Once the ring was on Janie's finger, and Winterton was writing a cheque, the conductor prepared to take his leave. But Winterton looked up and detained him.

"Have lunch with us," he invited. "I've got a busy afternoon, and I'd be grateful if you'd take Janie off my hands. Can you spare a little time to show her the sights? I'm sure she'd appreciate it if you could."

Janie waited breathlessly for Veldon's answer.

"I have got a reasonably free afternoon. . . ."

"Good!" Winterton slapped him on the back. "That's decent of you, and it's dull hanging about a strange hotel. Not that there's a man alive who oughtn't to jump at the chance of showing Janie the sights," he added gallantly, beaming at the girl who was pulling on her gloves. The enormous bulge created by the over-large ring on her slim finger seemed to have drawn both her eyes and the Austrian's, and when she dared to look up she wondered whether he could tell from the look in her eyes that her heart was beating extraordinarily fast, and that she was conscious of a tremendous sensation of relief . . . and pleasure.

Strange, tingling pleasure that ran along all her veins, and made it difficult for her expression to remain suitably demure.

Veldon smiled at her ironically.

"Do you think you can accept me as a substitute for Winterton, Miss Dallas?" he asked. "Only for the afternoon, of course. If you can, I'll show you the usual tourist attractions . . . the Danube, that is so seldom blue, the statue of Strauss, etc. And if you don't mind we'll look in at Vanessa's flat and collect one or two things that she wants sent to her. She'd prefer a woman to go rummaging about in her drawers rather than a man."

"Of course," Janie answered, her heartbeats slowing a little. "Anything I can do for Vanessa I will, of course."

His smile grew less pleasant, and they went out into the strong sunshine and took a taxi back to Sacher's Hotel. After lunch they sat for a while in one of the most restful lounges Janie had ever sat in in her life—so far removed from the bustle of ordinary everyday life that it might have been entirely disconnected from it—and sipped coffee and liqueurs, and then Winterton went off to keep the first of his afternoon appointments, and Janie and Veldon were left alone in the oasis of opulent quiet.

He looked up from the dregs of his coffee and smiled at her somewhat mockingly.

"Well?" he said. "Your guide is all eagerness to be of service, if you yourself are ready, Fräulein?"

Somehow she hated the way he said "Fräulein". It made her think of the days—only a very brief while ago!—when she had sorted new and second-hand records in the dimness of a dusty shop where practically everything else was second-hand.

"If you won't mind waiting, I'd like to change my dress."

"Of course." But his eyes ran over her very deliberately. "You look, however, very well as you are to me, and I can't think why you want to change it. You should know that that particular shade of pale blue suits you. It lends you an aura of youth and innocence!"

She felt herself flushing, and behaving awkwardly.

"Very well, I'll—I'll just fetch a hat, and a pair of dark glasses. After the comparative sunlessness of London I found the sun of New York a bit trying, and I don't think there's very much difference in the temperature here."

"It will be cooler in the mountains," he told her. A tiny cool smile played about his lips. "You'll have to persuade Winterton to hurry on the wedding, and then you can have your honeymoon in the mountains."

Suddenly her face blanched, and even her light coating of tan vanished as if it had never been.

"Please," she said falteringly, appealing to him, "I was rather looking forward to this afternoon . . . I haven't looked forward to anything since I left London until today! Please don't spoil it by talking about—weddings!"

Instantly his face underwent quite a miraculous change. The harsh lines vanished—even as her tan had vanished—and the aloof dark eyes melted like snow on mountain peaks. He slipped a hand inside her arm and led her towards the door.

"All right, my dear," he said quietly. "We'll play it a different way for this afternoon, shall we? We'll pretend we've always liked one another very much indeed, and that this is an afternoon to remember. Come along!"

CHAPTER XII

In the taxi, as they slid away from the front of the hotel, his hand covered hers.

"I have never really disliked you, you know," he remarked abruptly. "It was just that I . . . well, I didn't feel able to trust you."

She stared straight ahead.

"And now?"

"I . . . don't know," he replied, and looked moodily out of the window on his side.

But a few seconds later he was attracting her attention to the rebuilt opera house, St. Stephen's Cathedral, and other buildings of note. He told her about the opera house, and the tragic fate of the old one which the new building replaced. She gathered that he thought it far more important for a city to have an opera house than houses and flats and hospitals, but gathered also that everyone in Vienna—not only the essentially musically-minded like himself—thought along similar lines.

Vienna was devoted to music, and without it it couldn't live. That was a fairly unanimous opinion at the time when funds were being voted for the restoration of the city after the war, and immediately following the German Occupation; and as

she looked about her at the sunlit streets and
squares, the modern shops and offices, smart res-
taurants and hotels, as well as the dreaming Gothic
spires and fascinating Gothic architecture, Janie
realized that this was indeed a gay and inviting
capital.

It was a capital where a woman could have a
thoroughly good time, for not merely could she
window-shop for hours on end, but she could have
a beauty-treatment every few yards or so. There
were streets that recalled the magic of Viennese
waltzes, for they were named after their composers,
and streets where Brahms and Beethoven might
still have walked and looked scarcely out of place.
And, close enough to take a constant overflow from
the city, were the Vienna Woods, where it was
pleasant to walk on a summer night, and drink
beer or coffee in a garden beneath the whispering
leaves of the trees, and the far-away twinkling stars.

Max Veldon was not the type to enjoy an evening in a beer-garden, or even to suggest strolling in
the woods in the heat of the afternoon. But he did
instruct the driver of the taxi to take them to the
palace of Schönbrunn, which has an extensive park
surrounding it, now also for the pleasure of the
Viennese.

It was in the palace of Schönbrunn that the last
Emperor of Austria ended his days, and Marie
Antoinette spent a large portion of her girlhood.

Janie thought the palace had a wistful air as it stood out against its backcloth of trees, but she enjoyed wandering in the park, and she was sorry when Veldon said that if they were to collect the things from Vanessa's flat that she needed they must not linger any longer.

He had talked to her very affably all the afternoon, treating her very much as if she was a cross between a particularly earnest sightseer and someone very young and naïve who had to have everything carefully explained to her. He had bought her tea and an ice-cream in a kiosk, watched her shed her short light blue jacket that matched her elegant light blue dress and carry it with her hat in her hand—until he relieved her of both of them, and her white-gloved hands were free—and her hair grow most attractively disordered as the gentle breeze got to work on it. And when at last she removed her dark glasses and he could see her contented grey eyes, and the way the sunlight glinted through the trees and glanced off the golden-brown tips of her eyelashes, he felt forced to make an observation that surprised her.

"You are very charming, you know. *If* you marry Winterton he'll be quite a lucky man!"

She smiled up at him.

"Don't spoil the compliment by talking about my marrying anyone. You've given me a heavenly afternoon, and I'm very grateful. I never dreamed you'd waste so much of your valuable time on me."

He took her by the arm and led her in the direction of the taxi.

"It's odd how one occasionally wastes time deliberately. I've enjoyed this afternoon."

"Have you?" She looked sideways at him rather earnestly. "Have you really?"

He saw her into a corner of the handsome, glistening cab. Then he took his place beside her.

"Yes." He looked out of the window, and she had the feeling that he was deliberately keeping his eyes averted from her. "Yes, I've enjoyed it very much indeed."

"You sound surprised," she remarked. "Were you expecting to be bored?"

At that he looked round at her quickly. She saw his lips twist in the cool and definitely cynical smile that he often gave her.

"You and I," he observed, "have had fiery encounters, and even hostile encounters, but we have seldom enjoyed one another's society. From the little we know of one another I'm not at all inclined to the belief that we would ever bore one another. What do you think?"

She heard herself stammering, while his eyes watched her mercilessly:

"I—I don't really know ... but I'm sorry I told you in New York that you're a disappointment to me. You're not, of course. You're you . . . Someone very wonderful, who can give happiness to thousands, and it was I who was presumptuous when I imagined I was important enough to merit a little consideration. I placed you in an impossible position—between us, Vanessa and I have both done that!—and you were right to feel resentful. To resent me, at any rate. But it's over now——"

"So you feel you can be generous, and say 'Let us be friends?' " he murmured dryly.

She gazed at him rather sombrely.

"I'd like to feel you were my friend. There are moments," she confessed, "when I feel badly in need of a friend. Especially since—all this happened to me!"

"You mean getting engaged to Winterton?"

She shook her head.

"Not only that. All of it. Impersonating Vanessa, and having a taste of an entirely different kind of life."

He picked up her hand, and examined her ring.

"You can give this back to Winterton," he told her quietly, "unless you seriously and very badly want to marry him. He's a rich man, and he can give you a lot . . . but it won't make you happy unless you want Winterton, the man, and not his money. Do you want Winterton?"

She gazed at him in astonishment.

"You know I don't!"

He gazed back at her with a curious quirk to the corners of his lips.

"Why should I be permitted to see into the mind of a young woman like yourself? Why do you credit me with the power of knowing what you want, and do not want, from life, Miss Jane Dallas? By comparison with my advancing years you're a mere child, and as we're not even on the same mental or telepathic wave-length——"

"But we are!" she protested, as if she no longer had the least doubt about it, and now was the moment to convince him. And in that moment she knew what she wanted more than anything else from life, and the knowledge made her hand tremble as it lay in his. "Otherwise why have I always attended your concerts—whenever possible, that is —and why did I find it absolutely impossible to refuse Vanessa when she asked me to do something outrageous? I *knew* it was outrageous, and I knew I couldn't get away with it, yet...."

"Well?" he said softly, watching her.

"Because it was you—because you were involved —I didn't have the strength of mind to say 'No.' Honestly," she begged him, turning an eager, flushed face up towards his face, "it wasn't the clothes, or the thought of the trip to New York, or the temptation of meeting new people and temporarily leading an entirely different sort of life. It wasn't any of those things, because I was quite content with my old way of life, and I love Hermann Brandt . . . I mean," she corrected herself, embarrassed suddenly because she was making so many revelations about herself, "I'm very fond of him. He's been like a father to me, and I was happy working with him. It may seem strange, when there was so little glamour, but I was."

"I believe you," he said, almost gently.

"Do you?" hesitantly, drawing a little away from him. "Do you really? You didn't when I told you before."

"Perhaps I was being wilfully blind before."

The taxi had come to rest before an imposing block of modern flats, and she heard him utter an impatient exclamation as he looked out and realized that they had arrived. This was the block of flats where Vanessa lived whenever she was able to stay for any length of time in Vienna, and because he had instructed the taxi-man to make for it, there was no excuse now for telling him to proceed.

Although when he had alighted he held out his hand to Janie, and he kept her hand firmly attached to his own as they made for the lift and he swung the ornamental gates open for her to enter. There was no porter, and he worked the lift himself, and when they reached Vanessa's floor he produced a key from his pocket.

"This way," he said quietly, and turned the key

in the lock with an ease that indicated he had done it many times before.

Nevertheless, Janie refused to see anything significant in his familiarity with the lock, and as soon as they were inside the flat she was too diverted by the charm of it to do anything but admire it for a moment or so. Then the thought struck her that, even for a well-known singer, it was an extremely luxurious apartment, and she wondered that Vanessa should be so anxious to secure a contract when she could afford a flat like this. And she also thought swiftly of Hermann Brandt, and his little shop in the dreary corner of London that he nevertheless seemed to find quite salubrious, and she experienced a fresh kind of wonder. . . .

This was Vanessa's world, and she obviously didn't think Hermann would appreciate it. Or hadn't she made it her business to find out whether Hermann would appreciate it?

Veldon produced a list from his pocket, and handed it over to Janie. He didn't quite meet her eyes—unless it was purely and simply her imagination—as he explained that he had had a natural dislike of prying into Vanessa's private possessions, and he was very glad that Janie was there to do the job for him.

He stood beside the wide window of the sitting-room—which was so high up that it looked across

the roofs and spires of Vienna—as she went into
the bedroom to begin rifling Vanessa's drawers,
and her built-in wardrobe. But she had the feeling
that he turned and looked at her—that he watched
her very intently—as she disappeared and closed
the door.

It was a very simple matter finding the things
Vanessa wanted. There were some articles of cloth-
ing, which she had packed into suitcases, a set of
gold-backed hair brushes and a mirror, and a mink
evening stole. Everything of Vanessa's smelled delicately and subtly of her own particular perfume,
but it was not a perfume that appealed to Janie,
and she felt a little repelled by it by the time she
had collected all the things that were needed.

She was straightening one of the lower drawers
of the handsome mahogany tallboy when she came
upon a photograph lying delicately wrapped about
by a silk chiffon nightdress. She removed a fold of
the nightdress and saw that it was a photograph of
the Baron von Eisler, a highly flattering, very
masculine, photograph, and across the bottom of
it his name was scrawled—a simple "Rudi," and
nothing more.

Janie replaced the fold of the nightdress, and
then closed the drawer. When she returned to the
room where Veldon awaited her he turned and
glanced at her, just a little curiously, she thought,
and then came quickly towards her.

"You have everything?" he asked.

"Yes. I have packed two suitcases, but how are you going to get them to England?"

"Oh, there is no particular hurry for the things they contain, and I shall be flying back to London in a day or so. The cases will go with me."

"You are . . . flying back to London?"

She spoke jerkily, almost as if she was uttering a protest.

He smiled faintly.

"I'm always flying somewhere . . . London, Paris, New York. London in a few days' time isn't of any more significance than Milan will be in a couple of months from now, or Buenos Aires a couple of months further ahead still. I'm always hoping that one day there will come a time when I shall be more static, but that day may never dawn. I don't know."

"But you would like it to dawn?"

He shrugged.

"If it does it will mean that I have acquired responsibilities, and I am by no means certain that I wish to acquire responsibilities."

She looked down at the hand on which Abraham Winterton's engagement ring looked a little out of place. He followed her glance, and tugged at it suddenly.

"You must give this back," he ordered.

She looked surprised.

"You know I can't...."

"I tell you you must!"

"But—why?" The words came a little breath-lessly. "You have no right to tell me what I must or must not do; and in any case, we've discussed all this before...."

She felt him grasp her hand firmly, almost brutally, and wrench the ring from her finger. Then he opened her handbag, dropped it carelessly into one of the inner pockets, and closed the bag.

"There," he said, "that is that!" She felt the blood beating under the smooth skin of her face as his eyes held hers, and went on holding them. She had never realized before that they were quite so dark—so dark and deep, mysterious and compelling. He opened his arms to her, and he spoke huskily. "Come here! I knew when Winterton detailed me for the job of keeping you entertained this afternoon that it might end this way, but I can't help it!"

She could hear the blood drumming in her ears now.... It was a roar like Niagara by the time she moved impulsively to obey him and his arms closed round her, and she felt his mouth devouring hers. She had often wondered what it would be like to have his cool, cynical lips close to hers ... and now she knew. And they were far from being cool!

Whether he was capable of any cynical thoughts in those tumultuous moments she couldn't know.

At last he let her go, and as she looked upwards into his face she saw that he was pale. His eyes were gleaming, as she had never seen them gleam before.

"So," he remarked, "it is true you are not in love with Winterton. You couldn't kiss another man like that if you were."

Once he had released her she found it difficult to stand absolutely steadily, for her whole body inclined towards him, and she felt bemused by the turn events had taken. But in spite of emotional upheaval she was capable of reproach. Her grey eyes reproached him as she gazed at him.

"I haven't made it a habit in my life to allow men to kiss me. I only allowed you. . . ."

He smiled in a way she couldn't quite understand as he put a finger beneath her chin and lifted it.

"Because I didn't give you much option did I? And because you wanted me to kiss you!"

Her whole face flushed delicately.

"That's true," she admitted. Although her cheeks burned painfully she refused to lower her eyes as if either abashed or ashamed. "I did."

"Oh, darling," he said softly. "How deliciously candid you are . . . perhaps truthful! When I first met you I wasn't sure that you were entirely truthful, but a week has changed my views, and in any case you have truthful eyes." He touched each of them in turn with a long and caressing forefinger. "This afternoon in the taxi I was quite touched by the utter transparency of these eyes of yours, and I decided a man would always know where he is with you ... or should!"

He dropped her chin and moved away, pacing restlessly up and down the room.

"To get back to Winterton and this engagement of yours. You must break it off, Janie."

She waited, her heart beating like a wild bird in her breast, for him to say more.

"Tell Winterton the truth, that he's much too old for you for one thing, and he'd look almost as silly as I would if the truth leaked out about Vanessa." His lips curved grimly. "For I swear that at first you did succeed in taking him in, as you took quite a number of other people in ... mostly his own friends, at that party he threw for you the first night you were in New York. And if he wasn't deceived, why did he foist you upon his friends?"

She shook her head. It didn't seem to her to matter now.

Veldon continued pacing up and down, and she was vaguely fascinated by the alien way he spread his hands.

"He foisted you quite deliberately upon his as-

sociates and intimates because, once he had made
the discovery you were not Vanessa Brandt, he had
also made the discovery that he wanted to marry
you, and in spite of his position and all his money
a girl of your age might not capitulate at once if
proposed to out of the blue. So he threatened you
with exposure for myself, and no job for Vanessa,
and as I, also, had done quite a lot of threatening
you gave way at once!" He stopped to smile at her
understandingly, and more warmly than he had
ever smiled at her. "You hadn't much chance
against the lot of us, had you, Janie? In fact, I
think you've had rather a raw deal, and I must
apologize for offering you that thousand pounds."

"You knew I wouldn't take it, didn't you?" Janie
asked, gazing at him anxiously.

"Perhaps." Once more he returned to her, and
his hands fastened upon her shoulders. "But the
important thing now is that you've got to let Winterton know we're no longer afraid of him. So far
as I'm concerned I've never been afraid of him,
but Vanessa would have been glad of that contract. However, she can do without it. I'll see to
it that she doesn't lose by doing without it! And
you'll hand back that vulgarly ostentatious engagement ring, won't you?"

He lifted her hand, and examined it carefully.

"A hand like that was designed for something
much more delicate!" He carried it up to his face

and held it there for a moment, and then her whole body trembled as he kissed it lingeringly. "Janie," he commanded. "Look at me!"

She looked at him, her heart still fluttering like a wild and hopeful bird under the "innocent" blue, as he had called it, of her dress.

"Once you're free of Winterton I'll take you back to London and find you a job that will be much more suited to you than the job you had with Vanessa's father. You may be attached to him, but a girl like you can't spend the whole of her life in a backwater."

"What—sort of a job have you in mind?" she asked haltingly, as he frowned at the thought of her spending her life in a backwater.

He touched her cheek gently.

"I'm not quite sure yet. But there must be lots of jobs, and I promise I'll find something for you." His smile was intended to be encouraging, but it also seemed to her to be very strongly tinged with regret. And when he saw the blank look that invaded her eyes he looked away. "Perhaps Vanessa can help."

CHAPTER XIII

THEY both heard the unmistakable sound of a key turning in the lock of the front door, and when they looked round Rudi von Eisler was standing in the doorway of the sitting-room and regarding them.

"So Vanessa is still the centre of interest," he remarked, looking at his half-brother with a kind of semi-bleak smile on his face. "When Miss Dallas emerged as Miss Dallas I thought you would all do your best to forget her, at least temporarily."

"What do you mean?" Veldon demanded, and his voice was intensely curt.

The good-looking Baron shrugged.

"Oh, nothing. But out of sight is often out of mind, and Vanessa is hardly in a position to command the centre of the stage at the present time."

As if he resented the inference in this Veldon said just as curtly:

"I telephoned London this morning, and I telephoned London every day while I was in New York. Vanessa can't reasonably have cause for complaint."

"Oh, and I'm perfectly certain she is not complaining," Rudi remarked drawlingly, moving forward leisurely into the centre of the room. "Quite the contrary, in fact. I understand that, in addition to telephoning daily, you send flowers daily—or a local florist has instructions to deliver a daily floral tribute—and you keep in constant touch with her doctors. That, I consider, is being particularly attentive!"

There was a note in his voice that caused Janie to glance at him curiously, and then to wonder whether she could be wrong. For although she suspected that there was very little affection between the brothers, it seemed difficult to believe that there could be actual enmity. Not when Rudi owed so much to the famous member of his family, and Veldon could hardly be indebted to Rudi for anything.

"I telephoned London myself this morning," Rudi admitted. "And I'm delighted to hear that our nightingale is recovering from her operation, although slowly. She wants a few things."

"Yes, I know," Veldon said tersely. "We have already collected them."

Rudi glanced at the suitcases.

"So that's why you're here? I wondered. At first I wondered how you got hold of the key, since I have Vanessa's, but I suppose it's your own?"

Veldon's bleak dark glance lingered on his brother, and then he turned away.

"Well, since we've collected all that we came for, we'll go, shall we?" he said to Janie.

Rudi smiled at Janie.

"I'm almost certain I know what you're thinking," he remarked. "You consider Vanessa is very prodigal with her keys, and you could be right, of course. But I can assure you mine really does belong to me, for Vanessa is by way of being a subtenant of mine. But what Max's excuse is for practically living on her doorstep whenever she's in Vienna, and having the means of entry at all times when she's not, you and I will have to guess!"

His smile was so unpleasant, and so horribly full of meaning, that Janie felt her colour rise sharply, as if he had smacked her across the face. She realized, too, that there was a strange vindictiveness in his tone, as if something had happened that had affected him personally and aroused the strongest instincts of resentment, and she wondered how long he had been in the hall of the flat before he made his presence known by inserting his key in the lock rather noisily, and then opening the sitting-room door.

If he had come in very quietly, and been there for several minutes, he had no doubt heard something of their conversation before he opened the sitting-room door, and gathered what was taking place on the other side of the door.

But Janie didn't flatter herself that he was sufficiently interested in her to be, even temporarily, jealous of Max—in fact, since the announcement of her engagement, she had sensed that he was rather sharply annoyed with her. So the explanation for the note of venom in his voice didn't lie with her!

But the result of his venom made her move rather abruptly towards the door, and as Max held it open for her she passed him by with her face somewhat noticeably averted.

Behind her she heard the elder of the two half-brothers say coldly, as if it was an order:

"I'm taking these cases back with me to my own flat. When I return to London, in a few days' time, I shall deliver them to Vanessa at the nursing home."

"I'm sure she'll be very grateful," Rudi replied insolently. "Delighted to see you, too!"

The cases were rather heavy, so the lift-man was sent to collect them and place them in the taxi. Janie still kept her face averted when Max climbed into the taxi beside her, and she heard him say quietly:

"I'm sorry Rudi was a bit crude. You mustn't let any of his remarks upset you."

"I won't," Janie replied, with a crispness that made him smile very faintly as he glanced at her.

He reached for one of her hands, where it was lying in her lap, and patted it.

"To get back to what I was saying before we

were interrupted . . . I mean to do a lot for you,
Janie, and I hope you'll forgive me for being so
beastly to you in the early days of our acquain-
tance. I wasn't to know then that one day—very
soon!—I was going to feel regretful that my life is
as it is."

"I don't think I quite understand what you
mean," Janie told him.

He gave her hand another pat.

"My life as a musician, a conductor . . . it doesn't
permit ties. Only of a certain kind, and those
wouldn't appeal to you."

"But they do appeal to Vanessa," Janie heard
herself say stiffly.

This time, when he glanced at her, there was a
faint gleam of impatience in his eyes, but as she
was staring straight ahead she didn't see it.

"I have asked you not to be upset by anything
Rudi said . . . or implied. Vanessa and I are the
greatest of friends, and there has always been a
very warm bond between us. A very warm bond,"
he repeated, as if he was dwelling rather pleasur-
ably on the warmth of that particular bond. "She
is a tremendous artist, and I have an unbounded
admiration for her, as well as a great affection . . .
a real affection," he added quietly, studying her
face a little broodingly. "Vanessa and I are very
close, and I wouldn't want anything to interfere
with that closeness."

"Nothing is likely to do so, is it?" she asked, feeling her throat very tight as she managed to utter the words fairly calmly.

He glanced at her again. Then he averted his eyes deliberately from the wind-blown golden hair, and the one or two freckles, like the light dusting of a golden powder, that the unaccustomed kiss of strong sunlight had induced, and spoke with a kind of finality.

"No, nothing is likely to do so," he said with emphasis. "That is one thing about which I can be very definite."

Then, as she clutched tightly at her gloves and the white strap of her handbag:

"But I've enjoyed this afternoon more than I can say, little Janie . . . and I'm glad you didn't administer a very violent rebuff when I kissed you! It would have spoiled a very pleasant memory."

Janie felt sick. She wondered whether the slight amusement in his voice was linked up with the fact that, far from offering him a violent rebuff, she had fallen into his arms with an eagerness that would cover her in blushes whenever she thought about it for several months ahead.

Perhaps very much longer.

And she determined that never again should he be presented with an opportunity to make her blush.

When they got back to the Hotel Sacher she found that Abraham Winterton had returned to it ahead of them, and he was so genial and pleased with his own afternoon that he didn't even notice that the expression of his fiancée was rather strained.

"I met an old friend this afternoon, and she's going to make your wedding dress for you," he told Janie, certain that the news would please her. "I can assure you that a wedding dress made by Nicola Petersen will be quite something, for she's an artist to her fingertips, and will do you justice. She's coming to see you tomorrow morning, and I suggest you have lunch together and discuss the dress and anything else you'd like made. I've told her that it's *carte blanche* where you're concerned, and the sky's the limit!"

Max Veldon, who had followed Janie into the sitting-room of the suite Winterton had engaged at Sacher's, stood waiting for Janie to say something —she had the feeling that, standing immediately behind her, he was almost willing her to say while there was a witness that she couldn't marry Winterton, and preferred to go home to England.

But Janie said nothing at all.

The sitting-room of the suite was a room filled with so much luxury that it was almost oppressive, and as the heat was intense, and the heavy drapes seemed to imprison it in their velvet folds and silken fringes, Winterton strode to one of the windows and strove to open it wider.

"I've been feeling the heat badly today," he confessed, "and I must say Vienna's a bit of a cauldron on a day like this. I suppose it's because we're down on river level. If only we were in the mountains we'd be getting a bit of a breeze."

He turned to Veldon.

"About that *Schloss* of yours. How soon can I take it over? I don't want to rush the wedding arrangements unduly, and there are a few bits of business I'd like to conclude before I feel free to enjoy a honeymoon." He smiled at Janie, and put an arm about her, as if attempting to reassure her about the wedding arrangements, and convince her of her eventual security. "If the *Schloss* is available immediately, therefore, I can conduct my business from there, and nothing need be hurried."

Veldon stood studying him with the withdrawn expression on his face that always secretly disturbed Janie; but actually the thought struck him that the American did look tired, and there were lines in his face that indicated he was certainly feeling the heat. He was not a man who indulged himself to any extent, but a certain amount of inevitable soft living had rendered him a little less than one hundred per cent fit, and for a man nearing fifty he had been experiencing perhaps too much emotional excitement lately.

Veldon watched his hand closing possessively over Janie's shoulder, and for an instant he hesitated before admitting that the *Schloss* was ready for occupation if the impresario wanted to take it over at once.

"Good!" Winterton exclaimed. "I don't feel I shall really breathe till I get up in the mountains. We'll have a small house-party before the wedding, and if your engagements will permit I'd like you to join us, Veldon. Mrs. Petersen will join us, and perhaps that brother of yours might care to do so?"

"I don't know about Rudi," Veldon replied "but I can't possibly take time off to visit the *Schloss* Veldon. It would give me a lot of pleasure, naturally, for it's my family home, but I am far too committed to join anyone's house-party for the next few weeks."

"I quite understand." Winterton pressed impatiently at the bell that would bring a waiter and a fresh tray of drinks. "It's one of the penalties of your position . . . a servant of the public, and therefore no longer master of your own soul!"

"I don't know about not being master of my own soul." Veldon was gazing at Janie, and trying to force her by sheer personal magnetism to meet his look, and the compulsion that was in it. "I hope that I shall always be that, however great my servitude. But there are certain obligations I cannot ignore, and I have to return to London almost immediately. If Miss Dallas," he concluded, with great distinctness, "finds the heat of Vienna too trying I'm sure I can obtain a seat on the same aircraft for her. It's not too late to get in touch with the airport and make another reservation."

Winterton swung round and faced him in astonishment.

"Miss Dallas return to London? But what an extraordinary thing to suggest! She's coming with me up into the mountains!"

"I merely thought that, in London, she might find the atmosphere more familiar . . . and in a familiar atmosphere one can often think with greater clarity," the conductor observed smoothly. "However," with his eyes still on Janie, "that is entirely up to Miss Dallas, isn't it?"

"It certainly is not," Winterton replied with emphasis. "In future it's I who will do Janie's thinking for her, and make all her plans." He went back to the window to gulp in what little air there was. "By Jove, it's hot!"

Behind his back Veldon kept on looking at Janie. For the first time since they had returned to the hotel she met his eyes fully. And, also under his eyes, she opened her handbag and took out her engagement ring and slipped it back on to her finger. When Winterton turned and saw the action she smiled and moved to his side.

"I was so afraid I might lose it," she offered as explanation, and his perspiring face broke into a grin of approval. "What a girl! And what a delight to give you things! But you can be sure of one thing, honey. If you lose that ring there'll soon be another on its way from the jeweller's to replace it. So wear it . . . wear it and let the world know you belong to me, and you'll never belong to anyone else!"

Veldon picked up his hat and his gloves and made for the door.

"I'll see you tonight," he said curtly. "I believe we're attending the same performance at the opera."

"You're one of my guests," Winterton called after him. Then, to Janie: "Rather an odd chap, that. He knows very well I want him to meet a fellow from South America who is one of his liveliest admirers. And, unless he's forgotten, he's having dinner with us."

CHAPTER XIV

But Veldon hadn't forgotten. He seldom forgot
anything connected with music, and the South
American was a passionate devotee of it.

They talked opera while dinner lasted, and on
the way to the beautiful new State Opera House
they discussed in detail the lives of various composers, and Janie—who was concerned about
Abraham Winterton because, if anything, he was
looking more exhausted than he had done in the
heat of the afternoon—might not have existed so
far as Veldon was concerned.

He didn't actually ignore her, but whereas even
the South American broke off to say a few polite
things occasionally to—and look a certain amount
of admiration at—the slight figure in the dress of
moonlight net that, with her extremely fair hair
and her complexion of pearly pallor, made her
seem almost unreal, especially as her only adornment was her engagement ring, he deliberately kept
his eyes averted from her, and particularly the
white hand burdened by the enormous pearl ring.

The opera was one of the lesser known ones, and
Janie didn't enjoy it as much as she might because

the leading singer reminded her very much of
Vanessa. She was a little plumper than Vanessa,
and her hair was distinctly brassier, but from the
way in which his eyes remained more or less consistently glued to her Janie felt certain Max Veldon was seeing the same resemblance, and feeling
probably slightly tormented because it was not
Vanessa.

She was thankful that Rudi had not accepted
an invitation to be one of their party, for she was
certain he, too, would have seen the resemblance,
and would have looked at her occasionally with
that mocking smile in his eyes that told her he
could read her like a book, and he knew very well
how she felt about the conductor.

And, understanding how she felt about the conductor, he would also understand how she felt
about Winterton.

She would never quite understand why she had
put back her engagement ring in the sitting-room
of the suite at the Sacher, but having done so she
was not prepared to take it off again. She had come
to a decision . . . and it had only partly to do with
Veldon.

Winterton was the nicest man she had ever met,
and he had done her the honour of falling in love
with her and asking her to marry him. He was
much older than she was, and she was not even
slightly in love with him, but he was a man she

could trust, and a man she could lean on. He would, as he had said, plan all her future for her, and there would be literally nothing left for her to think about.

But, in addition to all these things, he was plainly not well, and she felt an extraordinary anxiety about him. She even forgot Veldon, and what had happened during the afternoon, as she watched the impresario closely, and decided that he was putting on a kind of bluff for the benefit of all of them, and that actually he was far less well than his strained appearance indicated.

About midway through the second act he whispered to her that if she didn't mind he would like to return to the hotel. She withdrew with him immediately, and without disturbing anyone, and outside in the cooler night air he seemed to revive for a moment or so. But barely had they reached the hotel than he collapsed, and by the time Veldon joined them—he couldn't have had his eyes quite so firmly glued to Vanessa's double (or was it treble?) as she had imagined, she thought thankfully, when she saw him walk in—a doctor had been summoned and was giving the impresario a thorough examination after having revived him.

He had been taken up in the opulent lift to his own apartments, and as Janie bent over him and undid his collar and removed the diamonds from

his shirt-cuffs Winterton whispered to her appreciatively.

"You're a good girl, Janie. I thought I was going
to faint long before I did, and I was afraid I would
scare you stiff. But you're made of the right stuff!
You don't panic easily."

He caught her hand, and held on to it.

"You won't leave me, will you?"

"Of course not," she promised.

"Not under any circumstances?" his tired grey
eyes searching her face.

"Not under any circumstances."

"Good girl," he repeated, and then, although it
was an effort to carry her hand up to his lips, he
kissed it.

Janie felt her heart swell with an emotion that
was new to it—an intensely feminine, almost a
maternal emotion—and she vowed inwardly that,
whatever happened, she would not fail Winterton.
He might have been unscrupulous in his method
of getting her to agree to marry him, but now that
she had agreed she would stand by her promise and
become his wife the very instant he wished her to
do so, if the doctor agreed.

All the same, when Veldon walked in, and she
realized he had come to be of assistance, she turned
to him with an instinctive gesture of relief. Her face
was pale and upset, and there was a tear like a
diamond-drop clinging to one of her lashes, and it

bounced off and rolled down her cheek as Veldon took her hands and gave them a squeeze. He looked hard at her.

"He'll be all right, won't he? I've had a word with the doctor and he says it was the heat that upset him. His heart's a little groggy, but there's nothing seriously wrong, and a good rest in a somewhat cooler atmosphere is what he needs."

Janie nodded. She went on clinging to his hands, although lying back in his chair Winterton watched her with a somewhat odd expression in his eyes. And when Veldon approached him he smiled wryly.

"I'm not done for yet, if that's what you're afraid of," he observed. "The medico says I'll live to be a ripe old age—and my wife," his eyes swinging to Janie, "will have the pleasure of getting to know my grandchildren!—if I obey a few simple rules, and remember that I'm not quite as young as I was. Not as young as you are, for instance," rather broodingly, his look resting once more on Veldon.

The conductor's smile at him was also inscrutable.

"You can give me a few years, but they don't count if you're fit," he remarked. "And for Janie's sake you've got to get fit again very soon!" He looked down at his hands, that were beautifully cared-for, and always struck Janie as an exceptionally attractive pair of hands, emerging from the pristine whiteness of his shirt-cuffs. "We'll get you up into the mountains as soon as possible, and I don't mind altering my arrangements to see you safely installed in the *Schloss*. The place is not on the telephone, but the inn is. I'll telephone the landlord and get him to deliver a message to my housekeeper, who will get the place ready for your occupation."

Winterton looked mildly surprised.

"That's good of you," he observed. "Very good! I know the *Schloss* Veldon isn't in the least primitive, but it will be something to have the master of the place on hand for a few days in case we run into any snags. How soon will the doctor allow me to leave here, do you think? And how soon can you place yourself at our disposal?"

"Tomorrow?" Veldon answered. "The sooner you get away from here the better, and I can telephone en route to make the necessary arrangements. Frau Karlsbach never needs more than a few hours' warning when I plan to visit the *Schloss*."

"Fine," Winterton murmured. He reached out once more for Janie's hand, and looked at her apologetically. "I'm sorry we've got to cut short your first visit to Vienna, honey, but there'll be plenty of other visits. And I'll take you to see so many places once we're married that you'll get tired of travelling." He smiled at her with a faint hint of wistfulness in the smile. "It's odd, when I'm really happy for the first time in my life, that I have to go and crack up like this. Happiness can't be good for me!"

Outside, in the lushly carpeted corridor that ran between lines of dignified doors, Janie thanked Max Veldon for returning from the Opera House to be of assistance. She had seized the opportunity, when he said good night to Winterton, to follow him.

"It was good of you," she said. "Good of you to spoil your own evening in order to come back here."

He frowned.

"I was Winterton's guest," he observed. "I couldn't very well do anything else."

"I know. All the same. . . ." Her eyes were big and dark with a certain amount of shock and strain as she lifted them to his face. "You do think he'll be all right, don't you?" she asked uneasily.

He stared down in a strangely concentrated fashion into her face.

"Would it upset you very much indeed if anything happened to him?"

At that her face flushed with a mixture of resentment and surprise.

"I'm not in love with him, if that's what you mean," she returned with a brittle note in her voice.

"But I can honestly say that, by this time, I've become rather fond of him, and it would upset me *very much* if he didn't recover from this evening's attack as quickly as you and the doctor have tried to lead him to believe that he will!"

Veldon caught both her hands, and retained them in a warm clasp.

"I believe you," he said. "And I also believe that he will recover quite quickly if he's not allowed to do anything foolish. And at least he's lucky to have you for a nurse as well as a fiancée!"

"I'll be happy to nurse him if it's necessary," she declared, looking up steadily into his face. "He's been extraordinarily good to me, and I'll do everything I can for him in return."

It was more like a solemn vow.

Veldon uttered a sound that was more like a half-sigh than anything else.

"Yes, I suppose he has behaved rather well towards you," he remarked, as if he was turning the matter over in his mind. "That is to say, he has treated you with considerably more consideration than one or two of the people you've met recently have done. And for that reason alone you couldn't give him back his ring—not now that he's a sick man!"

He lifted her hand so that the great pearl on her finger attracted the rays of light in the corridor, and gleamed with a wonderful lustre.

"From now on it's to be a serious engagement, is that it?" he asked quietly.

She nodded.

"Yes. A perfectly serious engagement!"

He lowered her hand slowly. His dark eyes were strangely regretful as they continued to hold hers.

"At least we had this afternoon," he reminded her, in an odd voice. "It's a pity that when we started out we didn't either of us realize it was to be a memorable afternoon!"

He let her hand go finally and turned away, after bowing his sleek dark head in front of her.

"If Winterton is fit enough we'll make an early start in the morning," he said more curtly. "But I'll ring first to find out how he is."

She watched him move away silently in the direction of the lift.

CHAPTER XV

In the morning the brazen blueness of the sky proclaimed another day of fierce heat ahead of them, but Winterton had had such a good night that he didn't seem to shrink from the thought of a long car journey.

He was obsessed with a desire to reach the mountains, and as he was assisted out to the car he talked to Janie of the beauty of the snows that lingered on the high peaks even in summer. And the thought of Alpine meadows, although a trifle sun-scorched at that season of the year, seemed to fill him with a surge of new life and cheerfulness. He remained cheerful all the way from Vienna to the hotel where they stopped for lunch, and which was a little less than a third of the way mark. After lunch, because he began to flag, they stopped rather frequently for refreshments, and to give him a chance to rest in the shade; and long before evening it was decided that an overnight halt would be sensible.

Veldon drove his own car, a long, sleek Jaguar that he had bought in England, and Winterton and his fiancée occupied the back seat. Mrs. Petersen, the Baron von Eisler, and another friend of Winterton followed in another car hired for the occasion.

Mrs. Petersen had made a pleasing impact on Janie. She was a woman with a good deal of quiet charm, whose age it would have been impossible to guess, and she avowed that she and Winterton had known one another for many years.

"And if that makes me old, it doesn't very much matter, does it?" she said, beaming at Janie. "We all have to grow old one day, and the years pass so quickly it's impossible to keep track of them, especially if they're very well-filled years!"

"Which yours have been," Winterton observed, regarding her affectionately. "You started from scratch, as the saying goes, and now you have your own Paris dress house and design clothes for princesses . . . if there are any left to design clothes for! But when you make Janie's wedding dress you'll be doing something far more important than dolling up a princess. You'll be designing a gown fit to be worn by the loveliest woman in the world!"

"There now, isn't that wonderful?" Nicola Petersen purred, as if she was really impressed. "Abe Winterton in love at last, and not caring who knows it! Wanting the whole world to know it!"

"And why not?" Winterton asked, patting Janie's hand. "I've waited long enough to find a

girl I could marry, so it's not unnatural I should
want the world to know. Janie doesn't sing, or do
anything clever, but she's clever at enslaving the
heart of a man. I should know!" he added, and
kissed Janie's small gloved hand with a gallantry
that moved her strangely, and made her temporarily glad that she had renounced an ordinary
woman's future in order to live up to his high
expectations of her.

But that was when they first started off, and
Veldon was very stiff and detached at the wheel
of the car. Although she could watch his hands and
the way in which his sleek dark hair grew down to
meet the immaculate edge of his collar, and
occasionally she could see his profile, too, she had
the feeling that he was miles removed from her
... and that in the future their ways would lie very
separate indeed.

She also had the knowledge that that was the
way he wanted it, and any half-formed regrets—
she knew she didn't dare to allow them to be anything other than half-formed, if the future ahead
of her was to be bearable, and not utterly unbear-
able!—were easily smothered every time the
thought occurred to her that by contrast with Winterton's benevolent appearance, Max Veldon's
aloof back was no promise of happiness for any
woman.

He was a man who was entirely sufficient unto

himself. Or was he? Did music suffice, or was his friendship with Vanessa the great thing in his life?

She was strongly inclined to believe that Vanessa meant very much, but for some reason Vanessa was the evasive quality in his life, and either her career—or some other man!—made the meaning of life for her.

But by the time they stopped for lunch Veldon's aloofness had thawed to such an extent that its opposite number created a tiny feeling of warmth about Janie's heart. It was Veldon who helped her out of the car and appeared mildly concerned because she was looking exhausted, and feeling very stiff. She had slept very little all night—facing up to the demands of the future, and worrying about Winterton at the same time—and on top of the heat and the strain of the journey it showed.

He took her by the arm and led her into the hotel, after Mrs. Petersen had preceded them into it with Winterton leaning heavily on her arm, and saw to it that she was provided with a long, cool drink with the minimum of delay. And when he received his own drink he smiled curiously and lifted his glass.

"All's well that ends well!" he observed.

If only, Janie thought, with sudden wild wistfulness, everything could end well for her . . . in the way she herself would choose! And then she found

herself wondering why he had made use of such
an odd toast.

All's well that ends well! But they were setting
out on a journey, and no one could predict how it
would end.

At the hotel where they spent the night—a delightful place, on the lines of a somewhat elaborate
hunting-lodge, built in the shadow of the mountains—Veldon still betrayed a tendency to watch
over Janie, since Winterton was hardly in a condition to do so, and she was grateful for his watch-
fulness after dinner that night when Rudi followed
her out into the garden behind the hotel, and tried
to assume a relationship that had certainly never
existed between them.

"I don't know whether you feel the same, but it
seems a long time since that night in New York
when we escaped from the others and went dancing
together," he remarked in a voice into which he
deliberately infused a great deal of slightly silken
warmth as he walked beside her in the velvety dusk.
"I wanted to tell you something that night, only
you wouldn't give me the chance."

"I'm not interested in anything you might have
to say to me, Baron," she replied, her own tones as
cool as a refrigerator.

A young moon was climbing into the sky above
a larch wood, and the air was sweet with the scent
of resinous trees. Not far away flowed the blue

waters of the Inn, and there was the roar of water
tumbling down from the heights to form a minia-
ture cascade below the hotel garden. Away above
the larch trees and the gabled roofs of the hotel
were the solid peaks that ringed them in, and
already the faint moonshine was glistening the
peaks on the farther side of the valley, and stars
were floating in the waters of the Inn.

Janie, who had escaped from the hotel to enjoy
a breath of the deliciously cool air after the en-
ervating warmth of the day, felt acutely annoyed
because the Baron had followed her, and the very
last thing she wanted to be reminded of was the
night when she had gone dancing with him.

It was that night, after she returned to her hotel
suite, that Max Veldon had accused her of en-
dangering his reputation, and she had sworn that
at all costs his reputation should be safe with her.

"Janie," the Baron spoke softly, "why do you
have so much to do with farces? Why do you con-
tinually get mixed up in the most extraordinary
sets of circumstances? This engagement to Winterton——"

"I refuse to discuss my engagement with you,"
Janie said firmly.

"But you will admit that, even in the interests of
self-advancement, it's going a bit far to consent to
marry a man who is not merely old enough to be
your father, but on the brink of becoming a kind of

semi-invalid as well? For I know his type . . . they live softly, and they crack easily. It's the fault of having too much money."

Janie ignored him, and turned on to a path that led back to the hotel. He kept pace with her.

"Of course," the silken voice went on, "I suppose it has occurred to you that there are advantages in marrying an old man? You might soon become his widow! And as the widow of a man like Abraham Winterton even Max might feel forced to notice you! Especially if you could pull strings for his Vanessa. . . ."

"Please!" Janie stood quite still in the middle of the path. "Do you mind if I don't go on with you? I find you—conversationally, and in every other way—unpleasant!"

"That," he assured her, without sounding in the least abashed, "is because I'm not Max. If I happened to be Max I could be as rude as I please— as abominably rude as only Max can be when he feels like it!—and yet you wouldn't refuse to allow him to walk at your side! That is the extraordinary effect he has on a good many women . . . but not all. There are those who actually have the audacity to snub him, and then he comes running!"

Janie looked about her desperately, as if looking for a way of escape.

"I'm referring to Vanessa, of course. So long as she remains Vanessa, Max will never look at another woman—certainly not seriously!—so if you've got engaged to Winterton in order to try and make him jealous you might as well break it off here and now. Max has had many lady friends —what do you expect, when he looks so attractive, wielding that baton?—but a girl like you couldn't hold him for a few weeks, let alone a lifetime. You may be attractive—we all know that Winterton has fallen for you badly—but never Max. Never, never Max," he added with soft, incisive emphasis.

Instead of trying to escape him, Janie looked at him with curiosity.

"Why do you tell me this?" she asked. "What business is it of yours, anyway?"

At that he smiled as if she had provided him with his cue.

"The reason why I may have sounded unnecessarily brutal is the simple reason that I think it would be a good idea if you realized that there *are* other men in the world—quite apart from Winterton!—who can appreciate a lovely, unspoilt girl like you. And you are very lovely," lowering his voice so that it was almost a caress. "So lovely that I must kiss you!"

And before she could prevent it he had swept her calmly but purposefully into his arms and kissed her in a very practised manner. Surprise, however, evaporated swiftly, and she struggled

free and dealt him a stinging slap across the face
just as his half-brother arrived at the spot where
they were standing.

Nursing his affronted cheek with a slim brown
hand, the Baron glanced with a curious expression
in his eyes at Veldon.

"Your substitute for Vanessa has a nasty temper," he remarked. Then, in the same tone, to
Janie: "I won't forget that, *Liebling!* You have
a very hard litle hand."

Then he disappeared in the direction of the lights
that streamed from the hotel.

Janie stood very still, gazing at her brocaded
evening sandals in preference to meeting the conductor's eyes. She felt in that moment that she
would have been far better off in old Hermann's
shop, and well away from beautifully turned out,
suave individuals like the brothers Max and Rudi,
for at least old Hermann had never made her feel
cheap and unimportant.

Even Winterton didn't strike her as such a safe
refuge as Hermann Brandt in those moments.

"I'm sorry about that, Janie," Max said quietly.

She made a little gesture with her hands.

"It doesn't matter. Your half-brother looks upon
young women like myself as legitimate game. We
haven't any background . . . you yourself once
mentioned that! And you yourself. . . ."

She lifted humiliated grey eyes to his face.

"Are you reminding me that I, too, kissed you?" he asked, with the same quietness. "But I didn't receive a slap across the face!"

She shook her head drearily.

"You didn't expect one, did you? You were aware that I wanted you to kiss me—you said as much!—and so you kissed me. I'm sure you felt you were being quite generous when you did so, and the only difference between you and your brother is that you kiss for different reasons. You out of the kindness of your heart, shall we say?— Rudi because he makes a habit of kissing girls like me, and doesn't expect them to take him seriously. You don't, either, if it comes to that, but I can't imagine anyone ever giving you a smack across the face."

He saw the unnatural brightness of her eyes, and the way her lips quivered, and he held out his hands to her.

"Janie, you know perfectly well that I kissed you yesterday afternoon because I had to! It was inevitable."

"As inevitable as Rudi's kiss tonight," she replied, and turned away. She started to walk back along the path, but this time it was he who caught her and held her fast. He turned her round, so that she faced him, and he said in a voice which throbbed, and which certainly should have convinced her:

"Janie, I think I could fall in love with you, but I could never love you enough. That's the whole truth! In any case, I'm not free to love. But you're such an absurd, impossible—improbable is perhaps the better word!—young woman that you had me intrigued from the start, although I wanted to beat you at the same time. You aroused my worst instincts, and my curiosity. Now I'm no longer curious, but my impressions are much more definite. You are as unlike Vanessa as anyone could be, yet you tried to impersonate her...."

"And Vanessa is ... a very special person?" as quietly as she had spoken before. "I don't mean as a singer, but as a woman?"

"Yes," he agreed. "Very special."

She nodded her head as if she understood perfectly, and then she managed without loss of dignity to escape from his hold.

"I came out for some air," she explained. "But I must go in now. Abe will be wondering where I am."

"And you won't let Rudi's incurably amorous instincts upset you?"

She looked round at him as they reached the house, with the golden light streaming out from it, and soft dark shapes like bats fluttering from under the eaves and winging past their ears.

"Not any more than yours upset me, Mr. Vel-

don," she told him. "There isn't really a great deal
of difference between you, you know . . . but in
Rudi's life there doesn't appear to be anyone
special. You should remember that in yours there
is!"

CHAPTER XVI

THE *Schloss* Veldon was perched on the edge of a dizzy drop, below which opened an enormous fissure in the mountains, like an angry gash; and at the bottom of the fissure a foaming cauldron bubbled and shot diamond spray high into the air.

The cauldron was overhung by a bridge which struck Janie as extremely fragile when she saw it for the first time, and she knew she would never dare to cross it, or feel the coolness of that spray on her face. She even had to avert her eyes from it after she had gazed at it as if it fascinated her for several seconds, and she was glad that, far below the cauldron, there were dark woods patterning the valley like needlework, and a succession of blue lakes opening out of the blue river beside which they had travelled on their way to Innsbruck, on which she could allow her eyes to rest, without experiencing any uneasy sensations.

She had discovered that her head for heights was not, at that stage of her existence, very good, but the mountains themselves were so beautiful that they acted as a kind of sedative on her whole nervous system.

She wanted to be out amongst them all the time, and not enclosed in the rather Grimm's Fairy-tale-like castle that was Max Veldon's family home. As a survival of medievalism it was most impressive, but the corridors echoed to her footsteps, and although the main rooms were luxuriously furnished, there were many rooms that, she felt sure, had remained shut up like prisons for many years.

When she lost her way for the second time trying to find a bathroom, and Rudi came to her rescue, she felt annoyed with herself. Rudi, however, directed her without anything more disturbing than a faintly amused smile on his face, and offered to show her the surrounding countryside if she had any curiosity concerning it.

"I don't suppose Winterton will be very active while you're here, and Max usually shuts himself up in the library and catches up on his reading when he comes to Veldon," he told her. "In any case, he's not a climber—and I am!" with a slightly superior smile. "The mountains fascinate me, and I've never been lost in them yet."

Janie gazed at him. She was wondering suddenly how she was going to pass her time in this lonely *Schloss,* and whether Winterton would object if she did any exploring. She was eager to explore, eager to be outside in the sunlight on the mountains, but her first duty was to her fiancé, and she must not forget that she had a fiancé.

She kept repeating that to herself as if it were a lesson.

Her first visit after breakfast on her first morning in the *Schloss* was to Winterton's room, and she found him very much improved in health, and also in spirits. The journey had tired him scarcely at all and, like Janie, he was full of enthusiasm for the beauty of the mountains.

"Open that window wide and step out on to the balcony," he directed her, as he lay in his vast canopied bed. "It won't give way, and the view will take your breath away."

It certainly did, and when Janie turned round her eyes were shining.

"You won't mind if I do some exploring while we're here?" she asked, returning to the side of the bed. "I've never been right up in the mountains before, and I'd like to climb and climb"—she lifted her eyes to a ridge of firs below the light powdering of snow that lay on a splendid giant across the valley—"until I reached the summit of that one over there."

Winterton smiled almost paternally, and patted her hand.

"I don't mind you taking a few country walks, but you're not to climb," he instructed her. "Not unless Veldon feels like a spot of exercise, too, and is willing to take you with him. I'd trust him," he added, laying a rather odd sort of emphasis on the words while he looked at Janie. "I'd trust you with him, but not with anyone else."

But Veldon, when Janie ran into him in one of the upper corridors, was not thinking of taking any particular exercise. He looked at Janie with dark, inscrutable eyes that gave away nothing at all this morning, and were even a trifle forbidding. He addressed her as if she was nothing more nor less than a fairly unknown visitor, and he a reasonably polite host—who had never made the admission that he could fall in love with her if he wasn't in love with someone else!—and inquired how she had slept.

"Oh, very well," she answered, not altogether truthfully. For one thing she was not accustomed to sleeping in a four-poster bed in a room that was large enough to be converted into a small ballroom, and struck her as terribly remote from anyone else. "And I'm dying to be out there," waving a hand to indicate the flowery meadows—and there were still quite a lot of flowers in the upper meadows, although the lower ones were mostly sun-scorched and bare—outside the window beside which they were standing.

He looked for a moment as if he was about to suggest something and then changed his mind; and the suggestion he made when it came was entirely different.

"Would you like to see my library? I told you

once that I had your father's book in my collection,
and it is there."

He led her into a room that smelled strongly of
leather bindings, although the furnishings were almost sumptuous, as if he had once planned to spend
a lot of time in this room. It was lighted by an enormous window with some mullions, and there were
some very deep arm-chairs, and a desk at which
it was obvious Veldon worked.

This morning it was strewn with papers, and
there were a number of books like account books,
which Janie suspected had been presented to him
by the wonderful example of a neat, hardworking
housekeeper who had welcomed them to the
Schloss the night before, and had all their bed-
rooms ready and aired, and an appetizing dinner
awaiting them, although she had had very little
warning to prepare for them.

Janie could see Frau Karlsbach presenting the
household books, and feeling a glow of pride because they were so well kept. Max Veldon was
lucky in possessing someone like her to look after
his home while he was wandering the world, and
delighting his fans with music.

He led Janie over to one of the glass protected
bookcases, took out a book and showed it to her.
It was her father's *The Great Ones,* and from the
way in which he handled it he respected the contents.

"Your father was a man who loved music," he remarked, as he returned the book to the shelf. "It's not altogether surprising that you got away with that little act of yours in New York, for you yourself are quite knowledgeable when it comes to the subject of music."

"Thank you," she returned, her lips twisting wryly. "I'm glad you don't think I let Vanessa down entirely."

He went over to a low occasional table on which there were several boxes of cigarettes, and offered her one of them. As he lighted her cigarette for her he told her:

"You never let Vanessa down. On the contrary——"

And then he broke off.

Janie sat looking rather lost in one of the deep chairs, and watched him pacing up and down, reminding her once more of an elegant caged tiger. From the frown that knit his dark brows together he had a great deal to occupy him mentally this morning.

Suddenly he stopped in front of her.

"I've had news from Vanessa," he told her quietly. "A telegram, which was brought up from the village this morning. It is imperative that I set off for London without delay."

Although she thought she was quite reconciled to living through all the years of her life without him, his news affected her almost like a blow. He saw the way she recoiled, and the sudden slight blanching of her cheeks. Her eyes grew wide with protest.

Without realizing what she was saying she said, "Oh, no!"

"I'm afraid it's, 'Oh, yes!'"

She sat very still in the chair, while he resumed his pacing up and down, over the beautiful Persian rugs that partly covered the highly polished floor of the library. Over his shoulder he flung at her:

"You'll be all right here . . . you and Winterton and Mrs. Petersen. Frau Karlsbach will look after you, and you have nothing to worry about. Winterton's making progress. Actually, I thought he stood the journey here remarkably well."

"Yes." She nodded dully. "He's staying in bed today, in order to rest, but he hopes to get up and resume a normal life tomorrow."

"In any case, if you want a doctor, there's an excellent one in the village."

She nodded again.

He crushed out his cigarette in an ashtray, seemed as if he actually squared his shoulders, and came across to her.

"This time it will be good-bye for quite a while, Janie. We shall, of course, meet again, but I don't think I'll be at your wedding!"

She stood up. She felt as if her knees had grown weak, and were not entirely up to the task of supporting her body.

"I suppose I ought to thank you for . . . for supporting me as well as you did in New York. Without you and Miss Calendar I wouldn't have got away with it as I did."

He smiled grimly.

"We'll say that Miss Calendar supported you, shall we? For some reason she felt very sorry for you right from the beginning, and felt that you deserved to be supported. Although she never actually said so, I have the feeling that she was highly critical of me and my attitude at times."

She looked down at her hands.

"You'll remember me to her when you see her, won't you? I . . . I should like her to come to the wedding."

He turned away almost impatiently, and strode to the window.

"Have you any idea when it will be?"

"Not—not really. But only this morning Abraham mentioned to me that he would like it to be . . . very soon."

"His impatience is understandable," Veldon remarked dryly. "But I would insist on a little patience, if I were you. You don't want to act nurse on your honeymoon."

Then, once more, he came back to her.

He looked deep into her eyes, and took her hands.

"There are other men in the world, you know, Janie. Couldn't you wait—for one of them?"

"And let Abraham down?"

"No," he said slowly, releasing her hands. "You couldn't do that, could you? And at least Winterton will be good to you. You'll never have anything to worry about."

She felt the words were a hollow mockery. Never anything to worry about. But never anything to be blissfully happy about!

All at once tears blinded her eyes.

Lucky, lucky Vanessa!

Veldon exclaimed sharply:

"What's wrong, Janie?" And then he bit his lip. "It might have been better for you, my dear, if you'd never left the protection of old Hermann Brandt!"

Frau Karlsbach came knocking on the door, but he sent her away. He returned to Janie.

"Janie, let's have a talk. Let's try and sort this thing out. Perhaps, if I put it to you. . . ."

But she was suddenly horrified by the thought that in another moment or so he might be confessing his love for Vanessa—avowing it openly—and she knew she couldn't bear that. She said hastily, surprising him:

"No, no! No, I don't want to talk." This time

it was she who turned to the door. "I'm going out," she said quickly, nervously. "I feel that I'd like to —to see something of the countryside. . . ."

"You'll be careful?" he warned. "You're not accustomed to this type of country."

"I know, but Rudi——"

"You can't trust Rudi. If you allow him the least bit of latitude he'll start making love to you again!"

She faced him with dignity.

"No one," she said, "is going to 'start making love to me' unless I approve of it. Rudi made a mistake last night, but I don't think he'll repeat it. And now I really must go. . . . You've got packing to do."

She started to race away along the corridor, but he called after her.

"Janie!"

She didn't stop.

"Janie, I'd like to say good-bye!"

She went on flying along the corridor as if she hadn't even heard him.

Later that morning she heard his car start up, and from a safe position watched it disappear under the ancient stone arch which guarded the entrance to the main castle courtyard.

Later still she put on some dark glasses and tied a protective headscarf over her soft golden hair and went out into the brazen sunshine that was bath-

ing the exposed mountainside. She was wearing
shorts, and a pair of sensible shoes, and she looked
up at the heights above her and decided to climb.

Gasping and panting—and it was only when
she had really started to climb that she realized
one had to be in condition for this sort of thing—
she at last reached a green plateau to which she
clung dizzily, while the whole world swayed round
her, and she wondered how she was ever going to
make the descent. But for the moment, having
reached her lofty elevation, she determined to stay
there, and to make no attempt at descending. The
thought of coming face to face with Abraham
Winterton's uncannily clear eyes—and, during the
last few days, she was certain they saw more than
they had done hitherto—was more than she could
endure so very soon after that final interview of
hers with Max Veldon, and the thought of talking
about wedding gowns with Nicola Petersen made
her feel physically sick.

Not yet, not yet, she said to herself, as she lay
very still on her ledge, her fingers clutching at the
short, sweet grass, until the world about her
steadied, and she was able to take in details of the
sun-flooded valley below her. The curious onion
shape that had been floating in the atmosphere
became the spire of a church, the walls and out-
buildings of a farm settled into shape and remained
stationary, and she was able to identify the silvery

clanging of a bell that had been making the silence shiver, with a solitary cow that, for some reason, had not been driven with its fellows to the upper pastures, and was cropping the burnt-up grass of one of the lower meadows.

It was all so much like a backcloth at the theatre that Janie could hardly believe in its reality, and after a time the utter peace of it all, and the silence, soothed her somehow, and as drowsiness stole over her nothing any longer seemed of such acute importance that it need worry her personally.

She allowed her eyelids to droop down over her eyes, and very soon she was asleep, the scent of grass in her nostrils, the incredibly blue sky like a canopy above her. And, no doubt because she had had so little sleep lately, she slept for hours and hours, and when she awakened the sun was low in the sky, and it was cool on the plateau.

Dazed and bewildered, she sprang up, and it was then that she became aware that she was not alone. Rudi van Eisler was seated near her, chewing the end of a long blade of grass as quietly and complacently as if he had been doing it for a long time.

When she asked him in confusion how long he had been there, he replied with an odd smile that he had been watching her for at least an hour.

"You looked very pretty," he observed, "lying there in those boyish shorts of yours." His eyes ran over her appreciatively. "Vanessa wouldn't look nearly as well as you do, dressed like that, but unfortunately Vanessa is Vanessa, and to Max that's all that matters, isn't it?"

She backed against a boulder, with both hands behind her. In that rarefied atmosphere, and standing up—while he remained lounging carelessly at her feet—she felt that he was very decidedly the one with the advantage.

"Max has gone," he remarked, throwing away the blade of grass and selecting another one. "I suppose you know he's gone to Vanessa?"

"Yes," she said.

"But he can't marry her," standing up and confronting her with a malicious smile replacing the languid one. "He can't marry her, because a couple of years ago she and I were married, and it was in order to raise funds which we both badly need that I hoped to compromise you and extort a lump sum from Max. You see, Vanessa's reputation is very precious to him, and he was never at all sure that it was safe in your hands. He expected you to cause trouble, and when it came he would have paid up . . . for Vanessa's sake!

"But, unfortunately, Winterton asked you to marry him, and that queered my pitch. Max, naturally, was never more relieved in his life, and the only thing he wanted to be really certain of was that the marriage would really take place. So he came up here into the mountains with you, and this morning Winterton told him that the date was fixed. You're scrapping the trimmings, and getting married as soon as the arrangements can be made. All Max will wait for now is a telegram announcing that you're Mrs. Winterton, and he's gone back to London to wait for that. Having seen you settled in here there was no need to hang about in the mountains . . . when he could be with Vanessa."

"But," Janie stammered, "if he knows that you're married. . . ?"

"He doesn't," Rudi confessed, smiling with much amusement.

"And this morning he—he received a telegram from Vanessa."

Rudi shook his head.

"He didn't. If he told you that he did he was inventing a piece of fiction, but if the fiction worked and enabled him to get away quickly, what does it matter?"

Janie swallowed.

"I don't believe all that you've told me," she said.

"No?" Rudi regarded her mockingly. "Would you like to see my marriage lines?"

"I believe that," she admitted, "because it ties up. I found your photograph in one of Vanessa's drawers, and then you had a key . . . a key to her flat."

"Max has a key, too—have you forgotten?" Rudi mocked her.

Janie knew when she was defeated. She knew when the whole world was against her ... and she turned and ran blindly down the path which led from the plateau, and although Rudi called to her sharply to be careful, she went on running—or rather, stumbling down the path, and Rudi decided to go after her.

But the knowledge that he was following her filled her with a panic she had never known before in her life. She couldn't bear that he should catch up with her and mock her afresh, and so, when she reached the point where the path to the *Schloss* diverged from the path which led to the bridge over the cascade, she went flying on down the road to the cascade.

Rudi continued to shout after her, warning her to be careful—calling her a little fool in a mixture of German and English—but by that time the only fear that possessed her was the fear that he would catch up with her. So, when she reached the bridge, she never hesitated to cross it, and it was only when she was half-way, and she looked down, that terror seized her—terror and an inability to move either backwards or forwards.

The bridge was so narrow that two people could not pass on it abreast, and an altercation of any kind in the middle of it might result in a disaster.

There was only a single wooden balustrade on either side, and if Janie pressed against it in order to avoid a pursuer... !

On the *Schloss* side of the bridge Rudi called to her coaxingly, telling her she mustn't take him too literally, and if she would return with him to the *Schloss* he would pester her no more.

"Let me come and give you a hand, *Liebling*," he implored, but she backed so suddenly that the bridge swayed, and Rudi held his breath.

Behind him a man put him aside with a rough hand, and Janie, who had closed her eyes and turned white as paper when the bridge swayed, opened them to see Max Veldon walking calmly across the bridge to her. He didn't hold out one hand to her, but he held out both his arms.

"Janie, I'm here!" he said softly. "It's all right, my little one, I've come back for you!"

And Janie stood absolutely still. When his arms went round her she shuddered from head to foot, and then she buried her face in his shoulder.

"I daren't look down," she whispered.

"Then don't," he advised. And before she had time either to look down or up he swung her up into his arms and carried her off the bridge.

On the path to the *Schloss* Rudi waited, but Max merely looked at him. Rudi disappeared as if he had never been, and the man with the sleek dark hair and the rather harsh face carried the slight figure in crumpled shorts half-way up the path until they reached a fallen tree-trunk, and on this he sat her down, and himself sat beside her.

"It's all right, my little one," he crooned, stroking her hair. "You're safe now, and with me you always will be safe!"

CHAPTER XVII

WHEN Janie at last lifted her head and looked up into his face she never would have believed that they were the same eyes regarding her that had so often looked at her with very active dislike. They were dark eyes swimming with tenderness and concern, and his hand that went on stroking her hair shook a little.

"Darling," he said. "You've a lot to forgive me for, but when I went off this morning I swear I believed I was leaving you in absolutely safe hands. I forgot that Winterton isn't very active, and you are. And even I thought that Rudi was harmless."

"He told me you didn't receive a telegram this morning," she heard herself saying, as if the words had to be uttered. "And he told me you only wanted to see me married . . . quickly! That you've been working for this marriage, and—and——"

"If I have, why have I come back now?" he asked her, taking her face between his hands and looking straight into her eyes.

"I—don't know," she whispered.

"Don't you?"

He went on looking at her, and the misery died slowly out of her eyes as the truth warmed her heart. She stammered again:

"Then Rudi wasn't . . . it wasn't all true?"

"Not knowing exactly what he told you, I'd say nevertheless that none of it was true," Veldon replied very distinctly. "Except, perhaps, that he's married to Vanessa. But I've known that for at least a year, and I suppose there's nothing I can do about it. Vanessa made her bed, and she must lie on it. But I've never been in love with Vanessa —I haven't even come remotely near to being in love with Vanessa—but I do admire her as a singer, and for a time I admired her as a woman. I knew that you thought I was in love with her, and because the truth seemed less admirable I allowed you to keep on thinking so. The truth is, however, that I valued my freedom to such an extent—or thought I did!—that I didn't want to fall in love with you!"

"And now?" she whispered, gazing at him with enormous eyes.

"I got half-way to Innsbruck, and then I decided that there was only one thing in life—one real thing—and that was you! So I came back to ask you to forgive me and give me that one thing I want, and luckily I got here at a moment when you badly needed me." His mouth tightened, and his eyes grew bleak at the memory of the danger

he had found her in when he got back. "I think
even Rudi was seriously alarmed when you
wouldn't come off that bridge, and I realized that
you couldn't. . . ! Oh, darling," his arms tightened,
and he drew her very close indeed, "when I
realized your danger I thought that I had come
back to perpetual emptiness, and I think I died
a thousand deaths myself. Every step I took across
the bridge was a nightmare, for I thought you
might attempt to turn and run from me, and
then——!"

She sighed.

"I'm too weak to run from you," she confessed.
"Never, never could I run from you . . . and even
now I don't blame you for wanting to escape from
me while you could. A man like yourself, dedicated
to a certain way of life, can't be expected to be
bothered with someone utterly insignificant like me.
And if—when you've recovered from the shock of
finding me on the bridge. . . ."

But he placed his hand over her mouth.

"Janie, I love you," he told her. He repeated,
"I love you. Do you believe it? Either," rather
more roughly, "you do or you don't!"

She moved nearer to him.

"I believe you, Max," she whispered thankfully.
And then, incredulously, "But you—you can't
mean that you—you *don't* want me to marry Abraham Winterton? For personal reasons?"

"For very personal reasons," he assured her, lowering his lips to her hair. "I want to marry you myself."

"And I won't interfere with your life?" turning her lips up to his, so that she spoke against them.

"You won't interfere with my life," he assured her solemnly. "You'll make it! And oh, my darling," as if he was taking a solemn oath, "I promise you that I will make yours! If you can put up with someone as—as demanding as I'll turn out to be! Far more demanding than Winterton would ever be!"

At that she broke away from him, horrified because she had forgotten Winterton. But he snatched her back into his arms and removed the last of her anxieties.

"Winterton won't really mind, because he knows you're not the least bit in love with him. And he wants you to be happy—he told me that last night —and if I can prove to him that I'll make you happy, then he'll let me have you." He stood up, drawing her with him. "Shall we go together and see him now, and then you won't have even a mild guilt complex to bother you?"

She nodded mutely.

"But first," he said, when they were standing face to face on the narrow mountain track, "I'd like to blot out something from your memory—

the memory of the kiss I gave you the other day. This one is going to be the forerunner of so many more like it that you may want to marry Winterton after all!"

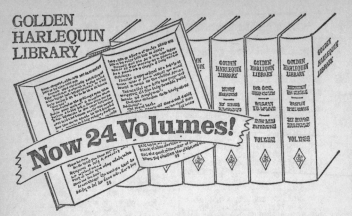

GOLDEN HARLEQUIN LIBRARY

Now 24 Volumes!

Harlequin readers will be delighted! We've collected seventy two of your all-time favourite Harlequin Romance novels to present to you in an attractive new way. It's the Golden Harlequin Library.

Each volume contains three complete, unabridged Harlequin Romance novels, most of which have not been available since the original printing. Each volume is exquisitely bound in a fine quality rich gold hardcover with royal blue imprint. And each volume is priced at an unbelievable $1.75. That's right! Handsome, hardcover library editions at the price of paperbacks!

This very special collection of 24 volumes (there'll be more!) of classic Harlequin Romances would be a distinctive addition to your library. And imagine what a delightful gift they'd make for any Harlequin reader!

Start your collection now. See reverse of this page for full details.

GOLDEN HARLEQUIN LIBRARY — $1.75 each volume

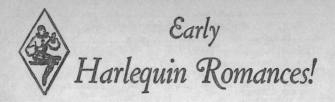

Early
Harlequin Romances!

HAVE YOU READ THIS SELECTION?

We recently made available some of the early
Harlequin titles which have not been in print for
a long time.

These include many of your favorite authors.
Check the list on the back of this page for titles
you have missed, and use the coupon below to
order them.

NOW AVAILABLE . . .
Some of the very first
Harleuin Romances!